LARRY FRANCIS

DERRIDA'S TOAST

Time & Place Prize Publishing

Chicago

Copyright © Larry Francis 2013

This novel is entirely a work of fiction. The names, characters and incidents portrayed in it are the works of the author's imagination. Any semblance to actual persons, living or dead, events or localities is coincidental.

All rights reserved. No part of this publication may be produced or transmitted in any form or by any means, electronic or mechanical, including photography, recording, or any information storage and retrieval system, without permission in writing from the copyright holder.

ISBN-13: 978-0-61-575010-1

Author Photograph © M.T. O'Connor 2010

A Time & Place Prize Publication

For Maria,

For everything

DERRIDA'S TOAST

ONE

That the tap may be open when it rusts.

Up the hill into the heart of town labored the procession. A crawling convoy of flashing lights and superficial solemnity. As dictated by tradition she rode in the first conveyance, a tribute. Two smaller vehicles, a sole driver in each, followed. Without complaint, she joggled over the uneven paving stones under Glohel's lone stop light. She stared expressionless at the cracked sidewalks and empty storefronts while her driver navigated narrow streets and inched around the tight turn by the mayor's office. They passed a *boulangerie* and the *charcuterie*, a Credit Agricole bank branch and Le Bon Bar. She did not hear the bells of Saint Peter's Church tolling nine. Nor was she concerned that few noticed her cortege.

It was sunny spring, a May day, in northwestern France. A Monday. The town of Glohel, nested atop the Black Mountains of west central Brittany, was waking. Monday was a market day, one of the two every week. (The other being Saturday.) By nine in the morning, on most market days, the fruits and vegetables, fish and meat would have already been on display. Those trying to sell clothes and handbags might still be hanging up their wares. The owner of the crepe van would be making last minute preparations before sliding open his squeaky window. A few early shoppers would be sniffing around hoping to find a deal before others arrived. There was no market on this particular Monday. This Monday belonged to her.

Glohel weighed-in at perhaps four thousand people when wet. And like most of Brittany, it was wet a lot. Also, like most everywhere, it had seen better days. At the beginning of the second decade of the twenty-first century, as recession raged around the globe, this once vibrant town was moribund, terminal. Countless small towns in France and elsewhere in the western world died of the same wasting disease, quickly and quietly. The cities, of course, were dying too. Everyone sensed it. But the politicians, the economists, even the philosophers claimed there was time to save the cities. For them there was hope. Glohel was caught in the middle: too small to save and too big to die mercifully. It was the perfect size to really suffer, just large enough for a protracted, excruciating death.

One hundred years earlier Glohel was on another track, a prosperous path. Slate extracted from the surrounding hillsides had made the town influential and wealthy. Booms turn to bust and when cheaper slate was found elsewhere, the local economy began to deteriorate, like the stripped landscape. Businesses left. People fled, many to North America to make tires for a new company named Michelin. In 1962 the last slate tile was shipped, the doors to the factory locked. And the railway made its final run in 1967. The tracks were ripped up and melted down. Despite the new processing/packing plant—frozen foods, breaded fish mainly—Glohel was withering and weakening a little bit more each and every year.

She came to Glohel in 1990. She was different. She was a gift.

After several nerve-racking minutes squeezing between La Tomate Pizzeria and the knee high stone wall of the car park, the motorcade reached its destination, her destination, the cordoned area in the center of the square, five long strides uphill from the memorial to fallen soldiers, a stone's throw below the post office.

The French, Breton, E.U., U.S. and Canadian flags waved in a semi-circle. Several retirees, a British expat or two and a few aproned shopkeepers stood watching. The three men, the drivers, without hurry, clambered from their vehicles and converged to help her. Somehow managing to appear both clumsy and dispassionate, they unlocked and opened the oversized back door as if for the first or the thousandth time. The onlookers appeared to share the same admixture of apathy and confusion.

She emerged from the truck bone white and stiff as a board, twenty-one feet long and lifeless. They coaxed her out, inch by inch. Supine and petrified, she was raised, without hurry, by rope tethers into standing position amid one or two weak claps of applause. She teetered a bit before settling into her usual place of seasonal semi-prominence.

Glohel's Statue of Liberty was back on her pedestal for another summer.

This replica of the original gift by the French to the young nation of the United States of America was a present from the Air France corporation to the people of Glohel in recognition of their flight(s) from home in search of a better life (in the U.S. or Canada) or their hopeful (and financially helpful) eventual return or the continual return (on Air France, preferably) of their descendants, and so forth and so on. Thus this Statue of Liberty commemorates the freedom to flee, permission to leave. The right of flight to greener pastures. Air France executives would most likely call it a collaboration. A win-win. She reigns, in spring and summer only, a Persephone in white plaster, the enduring, poetic verdigris of the original displaced by a fair-weather white, like something from Warhol. It's the Glohel copy, however, that should be a shade of green. For in reality isn't she a not-so-artful symbol of greed? Isn't she marketing cloaked as largesse? An advertisement disguised as a gift? She is bleached commercialism. Hueless, this Lady Liberty takes her cue from her environment. White wears two faces, always reflecting. In bright light she appears menacing, severe, almost angry. When clouds cast their pall she withdraws into dirty diffidence. She lacks subtlety. She operates at the edges, the ends of spectra, light and otherwise.

A miniaturized, blanched symbol of freedom, a crazy commingling of Franco-Anglo-American wants and worries, a dying workaday Breton town in the twenty-first century:

This is the town of Glohel in the department of Morbihan in the region of Bretagne in the country of France, a founding member of the European Union.

And this is where Larry Derrida came to die.

TWO

Dead men tell no tales but there's many a thing learned in the wake-house.

Glohel is where the story ends. His story anyway. The brutish, short, mismanaged and somewhat sad story of Larry Derrida. Death ends the story in most cases. It's a convenient place for a full stop. But the dead have no memories, no more stories to tell. So endings are, in the end, for the living. The dead-to-be may envision their demise, they may anticipate it, seek it out, will it, or even cause it, but they can't contextualize it. That task falls to the living. It is our onus. And we, the living, make endings meaningful by telling stories. We weave fantastic narratives and dress them up in colorful words: poignant cautionary tales full of fear, courage, misfortune, sympathy, love, loss, hope and hopelessness. Death (the end) is made significant because we give it life. Our stories exist and are made more powerful, more memorable, by reason of endings and beginnings.

Beginnings are rarer than endings. They are ghosts. They are equivocal. There is no chalk outline circling the beginning. No coroner's report to reference. Beginnings must be teased out, forensically reduced. And, still, *reductio ad absurdum*, the beginning is ultimately and undeniably a judgment call, an opinion, editing.

Larry Derrida's death began with his job. Or it might have started with his DNA. Or did it begin with his wife, Kathleen? No doubt she played a role.

It may be said to have begun even before his birth. Perhaps his parents sealed his fate. The only son of Howard and Jacqueline Derrida, Lawrence Francis Derrida, inherited all the troubles of the twentieth century in his blood. His parents were born in Chicago during the Great Depression (1930 and 1931 respectively) and came from the same south side neighborhood, Pill Hill, where the similarities of vicinage did not translate into socio-economic parity.

Larry's father, Howard, was the middle child of three born to Frank and Bernice Derrida (née Chatham). Frank came to the United States from France with his parents (René and Marine–née Maillard) when he was six years old. Bernice, the only child of Samuel and Elizabeth Chatham was born in the U.S. as were her parents, grandparents and great-grandparents.

The Chathams owned and operated a large, eponymous fur store on south State Street where Frank was given a management job upon proposing to Bernice. Howard did not want for much as a youth, although like most boys of his time he longed for adventure and chafed that he was too young to join the fight against the evil Nazis.

Larry's mother, Jacqueline, was the youngest child of Frank and Martha Kutka (née Doberstein). The Kutkas had immigrated to Chicago in the early 1920s from Poland. Frank and Martha, both purportedly Polish, met in the middle in a geographical and political sense as Frank came from Polish-Russian stock and Martha from Polish-German. Much of their legendary bickering may have been the result of this unconscious proxy battle for the true soul of Polonia. Although they both lived well into their seventies, neither, much to Jackie's embarrassment, learned to disguise their thick, Slavic accent. Frank struggled to support the family as an assistant butcher. Pretty Jacqueline daydreamed of nice clothes and travel.

No lineage is complete without rumor, in this case, as in most, bequeathed in fragmented, uncorroborated, susurrant stories. The whispers speculated that there was Jewish blood running through *both* families. The Derridas allegedly acquired theirs through an Algerian branch of the family while the Kutkas passed down muffled stories of Russian *mischlings*.

Larry Derrida's genealogy, his heritage, was, in effect, the admixture redux for World War II. He was an acknowledged combination of French, English, German, Polish and Russian. And do not forget the befitting, behind locked doors, tales of Judaism. His destiny, his tragedy and the pandemonium of a century rushed through his veins. He was fated for tumult, a twentieth century product in a twenty-first century world.

To make matters worse—or perhaps in an unconscious attempt to make them better—he married Kathleen Dolan who, if parental lore be believed, descended from ten generations of purebred Irish. Significantly, the young Republic of Ireland was neutral in World War II. Pure Irish, Larry would think but never say, as if there is such a thing. Are they Parthalonians, Nemedians, Fomorians, Firbogs, De-Dannans or Milesians? An almagam of them all or none? There's nothing purebred about the Irish, the mutt inside him reckoned.

So, is this where his death began? With the helical chains of mortality, the alpha alleles, the genetic splice of life. It's where *he* began. It is not, however, the cause of his death.

Larry Derrida died because he was human.
Larry Derrida died because of a mistake.
Larry Derrida died because of money.
Larry Derrida died because of his disease.
Larry Derrida died because he didn't fit.
Larry Derrida died because of his drinking.
Larry Derrida died because he was a fraud.
Larry Derrida died because of insurance.
Larry Derrida died because of Kathleen.
Larry Derrida died because he wanted to.
Larry Derrida died because the world had changed.
Larry Derrida died because he couldn't ask for help.

Larry Derrida died because he was born.
Larry Derrida died because he was afraid.
Larry Derrida died because of greed.
Larry Derrida died because he quit smoking.

It could have been any or all of these. An answer embalmed in overdetermination.

THREE

It's a dirty bird that won't keep its own nest clean.

The concatenations are endless. Larry Derrida died because he quit smoking. When he quit smoking his sperm count improved. As a consequence of his improved sperm count he and Kathleen had a miscalculation they named Owen. Then Larry and Kathleen got married. Next, Owen needed a sibling. So Kathleen again became pregnant. Then they bought a two-story yellow house with a green backyard and a one-and-a-half car garage.

Lines appear where we look for them. Begot by measurement. We are prosaic geometricians forever on a path from A to B. A single line will get you to where you are now. Select any memory, distant or recent, happy or unhappy, insignificant or meaningful, select it and start to connect the dots, and you will ineluctably find yourself down a very distinct and familiar path that is your life. It will lead you to now. Like raindrops on a windshield. It could not have been otherwise. It's reverse fatalism. A story written in water. All the dots, the points, the experiences, the influences, the memories, all lead to the here and now. There are no alternatives, no other options. All options are in the past. The future but a false promise. The present continually slips away, unnoticed, like a word unheard. Only in the past do we see the illusion of choice. Only in the past are opportunities missed or seized. It is from the past that we learn life's lessons and delude ourselves by asking, what if; never quite grasping that everything needed to happen as it did. The decisions, the twists and turns, fits and starts, rights and wrongs, had to occur just so. Just–so stories, indeed. It could not have been otherwise.

'What ifs' are illusions. The do not exist. They cannot.

"What if, God forbid, something happened to me?" Kathleen asked.

"I assure you, no, I guarantee you, that I will go first," answered Larry.

"You can't possibly know that. Things happen. The unexpected. Things we can't even imagine," she said.

"Trust me. I know."

Kathleen looked down and rubbed her belly. They were having the life insurance discussion. Again. She dismissed Larry's claim to divination by lowering her eyes. She knew better than to take the bait. Experience had taught her that the longer she waited the more ridiculous his hyperbolic words, hanging there, heavily, in the air, would seem. Wait long enough and she wouldn't have to say anything at all. Flustered by a silence of his own making, Larry would recant his hasty prophecies.

After a quiet minute Larry walked back his position. *Voilà!*

"Okay. Okay. I don't know for sure. Nobody knows, I guess. But I'm pretty confident that I'll die first," he admitted.

"And if it did happen, again, God forbid, wouldn't you want to know that the kids and I will be financially secure?" she asked rubbing her belly, unconsciously this time.

"Of course I would. Though you know when I die I won't know anything. It's not like I'm going to be floating about like some kind of jolly Casper protecting you all. This isn't a movie. You know when you die that's it. Nothing. *Nada.* Like before we were born. The void. So really this is about peace of mind while we're alive, not dead. Huh, I suppose that's why it's called life insurance, not death insurance."

"So don't you want us to have peace of mind?" she asked.

"No, I want war of mind! Don't be ridiculous. I want what's best. Yes, peace of mind is good. I want you to have peace of mind. Remember, I won't need it since I'm going first. But I'm already insured," Larry replied.

"Hardly," she shot, "your company gives you $50,000 and you have that policy your mother made you take out when you were young. I think that's worth about $30,000 or so. But, as you've told me a hundred times, the $30,000 can only be used on your mausoleum, right? So that leaves $50,000 for the funeral and to take care of the kids. Not much left after all is said and done. Is there?"

"I suppose not," said Larry, acknowledging to himself that he couldn't even begin to ballpark the cost of a new mausoleum. And I doubt they could find one used, he thought. "Don't forget. It's *our* mausoleum. It's not just for me."

"I know. It's *our* mausoleum. My point is that there won't be much peace of mind left after putting you to rest in *our* mausoleum. And yet again if, God forbid, I should go first you'll still have to build the mausoleum anyway and don't you want to have some extra money on hand for childcare and household help?"

"Aha," answered Larry seeing an opportunity to change the subject. "You don't think I'd be able to run the house without help. That's what this is about?" He folded his arms in mock indignation knowing full well that he would not be able to run the house without help. And without a great deal of help.

Kathleen smiled knowingly. "It's not that at all. Though, for the record, I think you can do whatever you set your mind to. This is about insurance. That's all. I think that it's important."

"I work for an insurance company. I know how important insurance is," said Larry.

"You work for a health insurance company. Health and life are two different things."

"I suppose they are," he said quietly.

Larry rose from the sofa and walked into the

bedroom. Kathleen followed him.

"What is it? What's wrong? Don't be such a baby, it's just life insurance," said Kathleen.

Larry sat on the edge of the bed remembering that he and Kathleen had been similarly situated when she broke the news that she was pregnant with Owen. How they had cried that first night. How their lives had changed since. Kathleen was pregnant again. She wanted to name the child Declan if it was a boy, Sophia if it was a girl. Larry thought both names were perfect, but he hid this from Kathleen. He was always hiding things from people. It tired him.

"It's not the insurance," he said.

"Then what is it?" she nervously asked.

Larry swallowed. She wrapped her arms around him.

"It's the process, isn't it? It's the knowledge. It's the information. That's the problem. Not the damn insurance. I agree we should have insurance. It's stupid not to. It's just that I'm afraid that they won't give it to us. I'm afraid of what they might find. I'm afraid I won't pass their tests. What if I'm not accepted?"

Kathleen thought this ridiculous. She loved Larry, however, and she could see he was troubled.

"If you're denied, you're denied. We'll cross that bridge when we come to it," she said. "I know you're worried, but I'm telling you not to be. Everything will be fine."

"Now it's you who can tell the future, huh?" He

waited almost a full minute before continuing. "Do you remember the scare we had before Owen was born?" he asked.

Of course she did.

As part of routine pre-natal testing Kathleen was given an HIV test. A week later, the night before Larry was to leave on a business trip, Kathleen received a telephone call from her doctor informing her that her HIV test had come back positive. She almost dropped the phone. The doctor went on to explain that it was most likely an error not a false positive per se and that sometimes every now and again HIV negative women test positive because the pre-natal test is too sensitive for the population group but that she should undergo and he is required to advise additional testing and should she have any questions here's the name of someone who could better explain HIV and the related tests and by the bye your husband should be tested as well. Kathleen put the telephone back into its cradle and told Larry. At her insistence Larry kept his business meeting in San Francisco while Kathleen made an appointment to talk with a specialist and to have more blood drawn. Husband and wife spoke by telephone day and night. Both were outwardly optimistic but inwardly prepared for the worst. On Wednesday the new test results came in. There were no signs of HIV antibodies whatsoever. Not a one. She was not HIV positive. She called Larry to tell him the great news. They both cried. Again.

"I'll never forget," she said.

"Well I've never told you, but for those few days I blamed myself. I cried for you, but I blamed myself. I was convinced that I'd made you HIV positive. Alone in that hotel room in San Francisco, just sitting there thinking, I convinced myself that I was HIV positive, that it was my fault. What then? What could I possibly say to you if I was responsible? And what if for all these years, even before we met, I'd been spreading the virus?"

"Oh, honey, but I wasn't. I didn't. You didn't. We don't have to worry about it anymore," said Kathleen.

"But I've never been tested. I worry," said Larry. "I think about it almost every day. What if I do have it? What if I have something else? What if we're not able to get insurance? What if there's something wrong with me?"

"Again, though I'm sure you're okay, we'll cross that bridge if we have to. It's highly unlikely that you are HIV positive. You should know that."

As Kathleen hugged him she felt him contract, his distress made tangible. There was more he wanted to say. She needed to pry it out before he could bury it anew.

"Is there anything else? Do you feel okay? Any aches or pains or anything? Maybe I can help," she offered.

Larry hesitated. Kathleen waited.

"Nothing specific, really. It's nothing. Well there

is this cyst on my tongue that suddenly appeared about a year ago. It's probably cancer. How much can cancer spread in, let's say, a year and a half?"

"It depends, though I'm sure it's nothing. What has your dentist said about it?" she asked.

"She said it's nothing," Larry answered.

"So it's nothing. Don't worry about it. Is that it? Anything else? I'll take specific or non. Come on, you've got to give me something."

Larry hesitated once more, longer this time. He couldn't make eye contact with his wife. He lowered his head and stared at the floor.

"Yes . . . there is . . . it's . . . I can't . . . no . . . okay . . . I'm not sure, but I think I'm losing the ability to walk."

As if debating the proper tone to take, Kathleen paused a moment before replying.

"Since we're married I'll assume that you know I'm a physical therapist. And, as a result, I just may be a good person to talk to if you've got a gait issue. So, what makes you think that you are losing the ability to walk?" she asked.

"I know what you do. Believe it or not I appreciate the irony. But it actually makes this more difficult." He swallowed. "Okay, here it goes. About six years ago I noticed that my walking, my gait, as you call it, had changed. Not drastically. Just changed. It was strange. No pain or anything, just the feeling that I couldn't walk the same, that my stride or something was off, more awkward. Out of the blue. It was different. But it's not like I run marathons or anything. It didn't hurt my golf game so I just figured I was imagining it and life went on. Slowly, almost glacially, it got worse. I didn't really notice. It was insidious. Then one day I discovered I couldn't stand on my tip-toes. I thought maybe the way I was sitting at work was pinching a nerve or something; so I changed how I sat, I stood more often and stopped crossing my legs. After a while I found that I couldn't move my big toes. I could move the others, not the big ones. The important ones. And at some point my ankles got weaker. It's like it's creeping up my legs. I can walk, you know. It's hard to balance and when I stand I need to lean against something. It's the weirdest damned thing. I don't know if people notice or not. I assume they do. You know . . . the man with the big nose syndrome. You've noticed my limp, I'm sure. I cut corners. I lean against things whenever I can. It's definitely gotten worse over the years and I'm worried it's going to continue to worsen, that I've got cancer or MS or a brain tumor or something. Maybe it's plateaued. I don't know. I should have told you before we were married. I'm sorry."

Larry's eyes were glistening with tears when he finished. He'd been carrying his fears alone for more than half a decade. He wept from relief. He was sorry and angry that it would burden Kathleen, but he was relieved that it was out there, vocalized and that he had someone with whom, for better or worse, it could be shared. He felt release and he secretly thought he'd taken the first step toward a cure.

Kathleen was relieved too. She was relieved because she now understood the motive behind his objection to life insurance. She was relieved because she could see how the confession lifted Larry. She was relieved that he, through his tears, had asked for her help. She was relieved because she was good at helping people. And she promptly convinced herself that she could help him.

Two days later, with four dry eyes and not one further mention of the limp, Kathleen and Larry sat in front of their computer shopping for life insurance.

"Are you sure you want to go with the same guy?" asked Kathleen. "There are thousands to choose from. We could probably do most of it online."

"Don't you think it makes sense to keep all the insurance products together?" he said. "Wouldn't that be easier?"

"Sure, it makes sense."

"He was out in the suburbs somewhere. Park Forest, Orland Park, Palos Park, something with a park I think. And I know it's Allstate . . . Tom or Thomas something," said Larry

"Here he is," reported Kathleen stifling a laugh.

Though the photo was black and white, Larry instantly recognized the insurance salesman who sold him the $25,000 policy two decades earlier. Larry remembered sitting in his office looking out the open window, wishing he was anywhere else while his mother told him this is what it was to be an adult. The salesman, Thomas, 'call me Tom', was flattering Jacqueline, 'may I call you Jackie,' on what a wonderful thing she was doing, chain smoking the entire time they signed the papers. 'Giving your son a headstart in life. She was. Yep. A head start. And your initials here, please. Yep. A head start. Something for his future.' Thomas McShane—Allstate agent—frozen at forty wearing the same ill-fitting hairpiece, the same wide, checked tie, the same unkempt caterpillar moustache, the same toothy smile.

"The guy hasn't aged a bit," laughed Larry.

"Don't they make them update their photos? It's false advertising. Look, there's the number. Should I call him?" asked Kathleen.

"Yes, go ahead," answered Larry walking out of the room to check on Owen sleeping. "Just let me know what I have to do."

What he had to do, what they both had to do, Kathleen learned in a very long telephone conversation, was to answer a few questions. And give them a blood sample.

"That's it?" queried Larry.

"That's what 'call me Tom' said," she said.

A little relieved, Larry joked. "Isn't the guy too much? I'll bet you could almost hear the hairpiece sliding on his sweaty head as he lectured to you on the comparative merits of whole life versus term."

"He is a talker. I'll give him that. At one point he asked if he could call me Kathy. I politely said, 'you may not'. And he didn't skip a beat," she reported.

"So all we have to do is answer a few questions and give some blood, that's not too bad," said Larry. "Is he going to email us something?"

"No. He said it has to be done in person. He said that it's part of their procedure, company policy. As he said more times than I could count, 'a million dollars is of a lot of money. . . even for Allstate'. He said that by meeting people in the flesh and being in their homes he learns more about them than their answers to the questions. He said he could be here on Thursday. I told him that would be fine. It is fine, isn't it?"

"It's fine," said Larry feeling his limp worsen. "What about the blood?"

"After he meets us he'll arrange for someone to come here and draw it. They do try to make it easy."

"I guess. But if he mentions my mother and calls her Jackie I reserve the right to throw him out, okay?"

"Deal."

Thomas 'call me Tom' McShane, his hairpiece and moustache both age-appropriately peppered with gray, straightened his wide tie and arranged a quarter ream of paper atop the Derrida's dining room table.

"I reviewed my files and saw that you already have a whole life policy with us. Well done. It's a neat little vehicle. I'm ashamed to admit that I don't remember selling it though," said Tom. "Different times. Yep."

Larry and Kathleen shared smiles and nodded.

"Usually we like to do this one at a time but if you don't mind I'll just ask you both the questions and we can get through this more quickly. Yep, quickly," he continued. "Since there are no objections," he laughed to himself, "let's get started."

They answered the requisite questions while Larry tried to steel his nerves and Kathleen tried not to worry about Larry. Most of the questions were simple or outright ridiculous, like 'Do you engage in risky activities such as sky-diving or bungee cord jumping? If so, how frequently?'

Twice, however, during the nearly two hour session did two hearts beat faster. The first incident was precipitated by the question about tobacco. 'Do you or have you ever smoked tobacco or tobacco related products?' After Larry answered truthfully, 'call me Tom' temporarily became a different person haranguing them both on the perils of lying on this particular question. "The blood test will tell us the truth. You can't hide the truth. It's better to tell me now. The chemicals from cigarettes stay in your system for months. If you've smoked, we'll know." For fifteen minutes he continued his aggressive warnings before appearing to accept Larry's answer that he'd quit more than two years ago and hadn't smoked since. "Well the test will be clean then and we have no need to worry. Let's move on."

The second and the most feared stumbling block turned out to be a non-event. It was the question Kathleen dreaded and the one Larry hoped would not be asked. 'Have you ever been diagnosed by a medical professional with any muscle- or nerve-related weakness or pain?' Kathleen answered first with a quick 'no.' Larry looked at Kathleen and grinned as he answered 'diagnosed, no'. He had been saved by semantics, rescued by his own procrastination, thought Larry.

Though there were other questions to be asked and answered and a rather lengthy discussion about the premature death of his father, Larry recognized that he would not be denied, not today, and his children would be protected, his family would possess the peace of mind they needed. He glanced at Kathleen and allowed himself a modest smile.

"These are very comprehensive policies with significant dollars attached," explained Tom placing a stack of paper in his brown worn briefcase. "We have to ask such questions even if they aren't particularly applicable in your case."

"Are many people denied because of their answers?" asked Kathleen already holding the door for him.

"Not really, no. Some answers can, as you would understand, influence the necessary premium, but no, it's rare. Once in a great while someone will say that they're moving to sub-Saharan Africa or some war-torn country or that they teach skydiving, but that's unusual. Yep. And we can more times than not work something out. Between you and me," he continued, looking around the Derrida's living room for hidden insurance spies, "most of the rejections are for HIV. And that always comes out in the blood test. Some people don't even know they have it. I'm the first to break the news. Yep. And, mind you, according to the law, I'm under no obligation to tell them why they were denied, just that Allstate denied them for medical reasons. But I usually tell them anyway. It's the right thing to do, I think. If it was me I'd want to know. Yep."

Larry took a short lap around the worry track and then broke the uncomfortable silence.

"So once we're insured and then die, assuming it's within the twenty year period, Allstate pays out. Is that the deal?" asked Larry.

"That's the deal," said 'call me Tom'. "Unless you don't make your premium payments. Or, of course, if you've lied to me. That would be fraud. Yep. Fraud. But you don't look like the lying types to me. I guess we'd have to pay. Yep. I think I speak for us all when I say that I hope it doesn't come to that. Nope."

"They even pay out in the event of suicide," said Kathleen. "That adds a new dynamic to our relationship, doesn't it Larry?" she laughed.

"Suicide!? Sounds like a bad business decision if you ask me. Suicide should be extra. You should talk to your colleagues at Allstate about that," said Larry.

"Well that clause does not become effectual for two years. The company actuaries trust that most people will change their mind by then. Yep. Timing is everything, I guess," joked Tom.

He left amid firm handshakes and promises of future communication.

Larry closed the door and hugged his wife.

"Now all we have to do is hope we don't have HIV or cancer. Whoopee!"

A few days later 'call me Tom' rang Kathleen to arrange the blood drawing. He also informed her that the nurse practitioner would administer an EKG to Larry—'because of his family history'—he'd said. Kathleen knew Larry did not like surprises like this and she felt responsible.

"But he said my dad's condition, because of what it was, would have no bearing on my medical history. He said that. It's like saying a car accident is part of your family medical history. It's crazy."

"They just want to turn over every stone," said Kathleen.

"Fine. Whatever. But this is really too much. We've had too much talk about death and dying. We've spent too much energy on it lately. Let's just get it over with," he said. "It's exhausting."

A young girl in green scrubs and a duffel bag in her hand pressed their doorbell. She introduced herself and said she'd like to begin by administering the EKG first. She connected a seated Larry to the machine. With all his might he tried to make sure his heart beat perfectly. The beeps and squiggles were beyond his comprehension. At last she told him everything looked fine. Kathleen gave him an I-told-you-so glare. The young girl in green didn't notice Larry limp (if he did) and she painlessly drew his blood first, followed by Kathleen's.

Larry Derrida died because of insurance.

The telephone rang and Owen spit up a mouthful of carrots in Pavlovian response. Kathleen motioned that she'd get the phone. Larry grabbed Owen, lifted him from the highchair and held him at a distance. Father and son traded silly faces for a minute or two until Kathleen said 'thank you' to the caller and returned the phone to its cradle.

"Here, take him, please," shouted Larry. "Your son is disgusting."

"That was Allstate," she said taking the dripping Owen from Larry.

"And...."

"And... we've been approved!" she reported.

"Both of us?" asked Larry.

"Yep," answered Kathleen. "He said they'd send out the policies for signature in the next day or two. All we do is sign, include a check and that's that."

"Great. Did he say how much?"

"He said they were still tweaking the final numbers trying to get us the best possible rates, but he said it would be about $500 a year for me and roughly double that for you."

"Double for me? Why?"

"You're a man. And an older man," she laughed,

handing a well-wiped Owen to Larry and kissing him on the cheek. "See, I told you there was nothing to worry about."

She was right, thought Larry. It had worked out. He had done the right thing, the necessary thing as Kathleen would say, and it had panned out. And now they were insured. Alone he might have let fear get the better of him. For the first time in a long time, since the birth of his son, Larry felt lucky. He was lucky to have Kathleen. He was lucky to have a son and another child on the way. He was lucky to have a good job and a comfortable home and a nice car. Taken together, in aggregate, it's not too bad, he thought. Not too bad at all.

FOUR

Two thirds of the work is the semblance.

Blue Cross Blue Shield, the health insurer of choice for more than one in three Americans, is headquartered in one of the Escher-like tower blocks dubbed the Illinois Center in downtown Chicago. This terraced collection of thirty-story mid-rises built on a reclaimed railway yard sits northeast of the inner Loop, bordered by Michigan Avenue, Lake Street and the green-brown, backward-flowing Chicago River. The fourth side of the complex displays no defined boundary; it simply vanishes into the mostly low-rise apartment buildings and retail stores slumping toward the east and Lake Michigan.

Illinois Center is a Miesian minimalist mess: a cluster of 1970s steel and glass towers with dark windows concealing gray innards, a black hole by the lake, home to, among other enterprises great and small, the American Alzheimer's Association, Blue Cross Blue Shield, Boeing Corp., the Czech and French Consulates, Deloitte Consulting, Edwards and Edwards Attorneys-at-Law, Giordano's Pizza, etc. The alphabet is fully represented in its directory.

Larry Derrida passed fifty-five hours per week on the ninth floor of one of these dark buildings. Every day, for more than ten years, he entered through the same revolving door, rode the same often out-of-service escalator to the same elevator bank, found the first available identically mirrored elevator, depressed the same Braille'ed button to the right of the same door which, dependent on traffic, opened forty seconds later revealing the same traffic-worn, gray-blue carpeted hallway leading to the same security door, keyed in the same four numbered code, passed the same two rows of executive suites, turned left to the same gray, three-sided cubicle where he stowed his weather- and workload-prescribed belongings in the same metal locker before he sat down in the same springy, mesh office chair.

Larry Derrida died because he was a fraud.

His job (career might be more accurate) was a fluke.

In 1996 Larry found himself back in his hometown of Chicago having exhausted his mother's patience and her money traveling throughout Europe for half a decade after dropping out of the English Ph.D. program at Loyola University following his father's unexpected death. He was a thirty-three year-old adolescent in many ways, one without practical resources or skills. He had spent the 1980s in study and much of the 1990s in travel. Though affable, intelligent and hard-working, his résumé was wanting. The city was not, it seemed, rushing to hire poetry critics. And that was about the only thing he felt qualified to do at the time. His mother set him up in an apartment while he looked for employment. Despite a vivid—human resource staffers used the word 'interesting'—and wonderfully grammatical résumé, Larry failed to attract any offers. Months went by. Finally, cajoled by his mother, he applied to a temporary service.

His first 'gig' for Manpower was at a greeting card manufacturer on the near west side filling in for a production assistant who was sent to rehab for 'a little drinking problem' according to the hiring manager. Larry followed production schedules for six dozen different birthday and sympathy card types, matching orders and shipments on an ancient computer monitor five days a week, eight hours a day, for six weeks until a clean and somber Estéban returned to reclaim his position in front of the blinking machine.

Larry's second engagement was with Blue Cross Blue Shield. It was the summer of 1997 and he was asked to report to the healthcare giant's human resources floor (number twelve) at the Illinois Center where he would be processed and escorted to the marketing department floor (number nine) and his assignment, which was to assist Jay Michael Collins, Managing Director of Brand Strategy and Marketing Services, who was short-staffed due to three concurrent FMLA absences.

"Marketing is about emotion and emotion is

about psychology and psychology is about perception and perception is everything. That's the only pearl of wisdom you'll ever get out of me. Other than that do what I say and we'll get along fine," said Jay. Appreciating the fusion of candor and brevity, Larry liked him immediately.

Ten years later Larry Derrida, Director of Brand Strategy, was still working at Blue Cross Blue Shield and still working for Jay Collins.

Through four promotions and a trebling of his salary, Larry's job description remained essentially unchanged: make Jay Collins look good. This was achieved without great travail for two principle reasons. First, Jay was good. He knew his business and was good at what he did; he made good decisions, had good instincts and worked hard. Larry provided counsel based on research Jay requested which Jay in turn either used or discarded without praise or opprobrium. Second, from the outset Larry understood he was in over his head. He didn't fit in. He knew nothing about marketing or branding or business plans or advertising or strategy. His colleagues were Ivy League products endowed with large MBAs, abbreviations and arcana. Larry's state school MA in English and an abortive year toward a Ph.D. in English Literature with a concentration on the Romantic poets didn't make the grade. His co-workers talked about theories and processes he didn't care to understand. On lunch breaks they dreamt of influencing decision-makers, while he lost himself in

Byron and Shelley. He felt he would have been mocked or shunned had anyone but Jay known his undergraduate degree was a double major in Psychology and English, not the inferred Marketing. As a result Larry was content to work behind the scenes and let Jay brook the occasional applause and the constant pressure.

With Blue Health Intelligence everything changed. Blue Health Intelligence (BHI) is a patent-pending proprietary aggregator of health information. In simple terms it is a behemoth computing system capable of collecting and parsing claims data from the entire Blues organization. In other words it catalogues each and every piece of health information collected by any of the Blue Cross Blue Shield Plans in the United States. It contains data on broken legs in Arizona and heart transplants in Idaho. It compiles the statistics on bariatric surgeries in Florida and orthotics in Texas. It stores every claims-related incident from over one hundred million people. Year in and year out. In essence it is the comprehensive collective memory of the nation's healthcare system. It is medical big data.

From its inception BHI was big and it needed a big name. Jay Collins and his team outsourced the creation and vetting of potential names to three of the country's leading branding experts. Each group presented three suggestions. They submitted names like $Blue^2$, Intellix, 21st Century Blue and HealthLogic. Jay was not impressed. And then Larry in a casual aside one late afternoon in Jay's office suggested Blue Health Intelligence. Jay loved it and included it with the nine others in the decision-point memorandum to the SVP of the division and the CEO. The CEO selected Blue Health Intelligence. Jay insisted Larry get the recognition he deserved for his contribution.

"A win like this doesn't come around every day. I won't be around forever, you know. This is a competitive place. No one is safe. Take the credit. You've earned it. Anyway, it won't last long. That I promise."

Larry was made a Director and put in charge of the narrative marketing team for BHI. His cloak of insignificance removed, Larry played his new role to the best of his abilities. His team, a team he assembled and managed, was charged with identifying key questions BHI could answer. What did they want to know from big data? These questions, in turn, would be translated into logarithms by IT and the system would do the rest. He still reported to Jay who was made Executive Director, but for the first time at Blue Cross Blue Shield Larry was held accountable. He was no longer able to hide behind his boss. The new title and larger paycheck came with more freedom chained to greater responsibility. Forced to give presentations he saw his limp worsen. People began asking questions, all manner of questions. He was invited to meeting after meeting. They asked for his advice. They valued his opinion. He had to fire people and reprimand others. He worked harder. He logged more hours in the office. His team thrived.

And he earned more praise. But through it all his lack of pedigree skulked meekly like a wrongfully imprisoned accountant caught up in a jailbreak.

Successful careers need at least a soupçon of charlatanism. It's human nature. We are a species bewitched by confidence. A bit of braggadocio and swagger, a whiff of self-importance, these are perceived as positive attributes, strengths. And while there are always exceptions to the rule, the 'softer' the job the more important this appearance of self-assurance becomes. Politicians, preachers, C-Level executives and salesmen are soft. Engineers, programmers and physicians are hard. Larry Derrida's job was soft while Kathleen Derrida's was hard. We seem to have created an absurd inverse relationship between self-promotion and expertise, between talk and action. A congressman is compelled to clamor about the merits of voting against the bill before voting for it, yet when an orthopedic surgeon repairs a ruptured Achilles tendon, he requires no pronouncement, no spin, to reattach it correctly to the calcaneus.

"How's Roger the cop doing? Is he walking yet?" Dr. Stanley Archer asked.

"We should be able to remove the CAM walker next week," answered Kathleen. "He's been terribly compliant. Still a little antalgic, but that's to be expected. Barring any setbacks, he'll be right as rain in a few weeks."

"Happy to hear it. With the world's best surgeon and best PT I expected nothing less," he said. "And there will not be any setbacks."

Dr. Archer was a really good surgeon, thought Kathleen. He wasn't the best, but he was quite good. She almost never encountered complications with his patients. And she could not remember a single case of infection. She silently wished the others in the NOC practice were as talented. That's not life though, is it? she mused.

The Northwestern Orthopedic Clinic (NOC) was a good place for Kathleen to be. Located in the historic twenty-nine-story art-deco building—when it was completed in 1926 it was the largest building in the world—at 680 North Lake Shore Drive, comfortably situated between Lake Michigan and Northwestern Hospital, the clinic was affiliated, as the name suggests, with Northwestern Hospital and was group-owned by the doctors in a private orthopedic practice but staffed by PhysiCo, an independent physical therapy group with more than thirty-five clinics throughout Chicagoland. Kathleen was paid by PhysiCo, but she worked for NOC. It was an unusual set-up.

Kathleen had been with PhysiCo for eleven years. She'd seen it grow steadily from the original two clinics. In the beginning eight therapists, including the owner, John, shuttled from clinic to clinic. She clocked eighty hour work weeks and watched the company grow so large that she was forced to navigate a massive human resources department just to have a chat with John. At one point, not long before she became pregnant with Owen, she was even in charge of her own clinic and had an opportunity for partnership in the company. Life had other plans, however.

  She pulled up Roger's SOAP chart. She smiled. He thought he'd been shot in the calf, she remembered. The sixty-three year-old ex-cop, supplementing his city pension by checking IDs at The Art Institute, had ruptured his Achilles tendon trying to apprehend a fleeing purse snatcher in front of the museum. Kathleen had seen so many of these injuries she could almost hear the pop and feel the pain. He'll be walking in no time, she told herself. How many times have I done this? she thought. How many people have I touched? Proprioception drills, isometric exercises, eccentric exercises, improving core strength, arms, legs, necks, shoulders, faces in pain, faces talking, laughing and crying faces. It always amazed her how patients bonded so quickly, how much of their personal lives they shared with her, a total stranger. They hadn't taught her that at Trinity. Those college courses seemed as far away as her birthplace.

  After almost twenty years as a practicing therapist she knew how the system worked and how she wanted it to work. She preferred being close to the 'docs' as she called them. It made it easier to do her job. NOC had been the right place for her after

Declan was born. She liked to work; she needed to work, but just a bit, just a taste . . . for herself.

The two days a week at the clinic kept her satisfied, professionally, intellectually and socially. She'd found a healthy balance. When she became pregnant for the third time in six years, however, Kathleen was compelled to question her evanescing career.

But 2008 was gravid for other reasons too. Lehman Brothers, the fourth largest investment bank in the country, was forced to declare bankruptcy sending the world's banking system into crisis, the first thunderous crack in the dam of western capitalism. And Barack Obama, a mixed-race, freshman senator from Illinois, was elected the forty-fourth President of the United States in large part due to his call for change and, in particular, his plan for affordable healthcare for all. These external events would soon be felt by the Derridas and millions of other people around the globe.

It was too cold for a lake cruise. The Strategic Services Division's Event Planning Committee had questioned the October date earlier in the year only to have their concerns vetoed by the Senior Vice President. One hundred and thirteen Blue Cross Blue Shield employees crammed into the glass-enclosed dining room and pretended to socialize with the same people they saw at work every day. The boat's upper deck, exposed to the frigid autumn air, was vacant.

Larry circumspectly made his way around the small room. The sway of the ship played havoc with his poor balance. He stopped to lean against a wall or a chair whenever he could. As he passed the inner circle, the most senior officers in the division, he overheard the SVP crowing that 'maybe now that the bankers are the new bad guys, they'll ease up on us.' A sycophantic chorus echoed the cackle. Squeezed by the crowd he climbed the stairs to the upper deck and for the first time in over an hour sat down. He was alone and cold, but secure. Every few minutes someone would join him long enough to comment on the chill before returning below. After a time Larry no longer felt his toes and found it difficult to flex his ankles. He sat and shivered.

The ship turned back toward the city. Larry was joined by two colleagues from the marketing team; soon others came on deck to watch the skyline grow as the ship approached Navy Pier. Larry's legs were numb. He worried that he would not have the ability to stand, let alone disembark. He tried to stretch his Achilles tendons and begged his ankle strength to return. Jay saw him flexing and asked what was wrong.

"Oh, I turned my ankle the other day and the cold must have made it worse. I'll be fine," Larry said. It was the first time he'd ever lied to Jay.

"You shouldn't have been out here so long. It was nice and toasty below. A little too for that matter," said Jay with a wink.

The boat docked. Larry watched and waited for the inner circle to go ashore before he climbed off. He limped down the long pier toward the taxi rank. His feet flopped flat. Every step was a struggle. Out of nowhere Jay ran up and offered a shoulder.
"You should get that checked out," he said thumping the top of the taxi. "See you tomorrow."

Larry conquered the stairhead of their home, turned his key and dragged himself across the threshold. The boys are asleep whispered Kathleen wordlessly. Larry nodded and fell into the nearest chair.

"How was the work cruise? Uh oh. What's wrong?" asked Kathleen.

"It's worse. It's definitely getting worse," sighed Larry. "The cold made it way worse. Can the cold do that? I could barely walk. I think I need to see somebody." He paused as if to reassure himself. "Do me a favor and ask around at Northwestern and get me an appointment with the best neurologist you can find, okay?"

"Oh honey, of course. Can I get you anything? I'll take care of it. I am proud of you. First though you should see an internist, but don't worry, I'll take care of that too. I'm happy you want help. You'll be happier. I promise," she said, reaching for his hand.

FIVE

May those that love us, love us; and those that don't love us, may God turn their hearts; if He can't turn their hearts, then may He turn their ankles, so we'll know them by their limp.

He over-tipped the cabbie, closed the door and hobbled up to the ninth floor still sore, leg muscles throbbing and twitching; twelve tiny crosses of blueblack ink hidden beneath his suit marked where he'd been pierced. I am spending far too much on taxis lately, thought Larry.

Throughout the afternoon he tried to focus on work. His tormented lower limbs relaxed. The pain decreased. His vulnerability vanished. The agony of the NCV and EMG tests was left behind, replaced by relief and then a budding hope. He felt rejuvenated by a nascent sense of accomplishment, soothed by a pinch of pride. This was a big deal for Larry: it took him a real effort to submit to the tests, to capitulate, to give up control. It had not been pleasant, but it had been necessary. To get this far, to accept that something was wrong and then agree to be tested, was in itself a triumph a decade in the making. And now it was up to them, the doctors, the specialists. Surely they had seen cases like his before. They would tell him what was wrong. They would diagnose him. They would label him. They would have to. That much he also knew. But at least he would have a name, something he could call it, something tangible to face, something to oppose, something to battle against or surrender to.

Larry had to first run the gauntlet of American medicine's labyrinth in order to even qualify for the tests. It started with a visit to the internist, the baby-faced and affable Dr. Youklis. It was Larry's first check-up in fifteen years and the first time he'd ever been examined by someone younger.

"So what brings you here today?" asked the doctor.

Larry explained his leg issues and also confessed that it had been too long since he'd had a physical. Dr. Youklis nodded, uttered 'hmm' twice and 'really' once, but mostly let Larry talk.

"Okay, then, let's take a look," said the doctor when he was sure Larry had finished.

Breezy and accommodating, Dr. Youklis tapped, poked and measured. He listened to Larry's heart and lungs. The two men chatted about family, work and leisure. They each had two boys and another child on the way. He asked Larry about his diet and if he always wore sunscreen.

"We'll give your blood a good work-up. Check for Lyme Disease, that sort of thing. Everything else looks pretty good. There's just one last thing," said the doctor slipping a rubber glove over the tips of his fingers.

"Oh no, thank you, but no," said Larry. "We don't need to get that physical."

"Are you sure?" asked Dr. Youklis. "We want to be completely thorough."

"Oh yeah, I'm sure," said Larry.

"Next time then," he said taking off the glove.

"We'll see," laughed Larry.

"Have you already selected a neurologist?" asked the doctor clicking a mouse.

"My wife, who works at NOC, talked to a neurologist who recommended Dr. Mendelson," answered Larry dressing.

Dr. Youklis checked the Northwestern physician directory on the computer. "Yeah, that's probably the right guy."

"If there are no issues with the blood work, I'll just mail you the results. It should take about a week or so."

"Thank you," said Larry as a buxom blonde nurse materialized next to him.

"Eva will take you to have your blood drawn," smiled the doctor.

Kathleen read and interpreted the numbers and levels. The tests were negative in a positive sense:

Lyme Disease, negative;

Blood glucose, normal: "That means you're not diabetic," she commented;

Heavy metals, negative;

Blood pressure: excellent, "Wow, 117 over 70, that's great!"

"He writes here that your Vitamin D level, although in the normal range, is a little on the low side so you should take supplements."

"Either it's normal or it's low. It can't be both," stated Larry.

"It's normal, but it's on the lower end of normal," countered Kathleen.

"They always have to find something, even when their tests can't," said Larry. "That's their business model, isn't it? I'm normal, but I could be a 'better' normal if I buy their pills. Everyone has to be normal normal, huh? Not me, thank you very much. I'll stay exceptional if you don't mind. I don't know how you can stand to work with these people," he said thinking he went a tad too far with his final sentence.

Kathleen ignored him.

"Is that it?" asked Larry. "Nothing about my legs? Nothing about my mystery malady?"

"Nope. Not in here. But they'll send these over to your neurologist."

"My neurologist!? I haven't even met the guy yet. Neurologist-to-be, maybe, or how about neurologist-in-waiting?"

For the second time in two weeks he sat half-naked on a cold table while someone measured the pressure of his blood. All comparisons ended there. The pretty pastels and soothing nature photographs of Dr. Youklis' office were replaced by the stark lighting and ugly brown walls of the hospital. The only color in the room came from the fact sheets tacked to a solitary bulletin board. Larry read the titles—'Coping with ALS?' and 'Do I Have a Brain Tumor?' and 'Living with MS'—with wide eyes as the black band of the sphygmomanometer tightened around his arm.

"It's a little high," said the nurse.

"White coat syndrome," joked Larry.

"Right," she said without smiling. "The doctor will be in in a minute."

Northwestern Hospital is a teaching hospital. Where doctors like to travel in packs. Larry got three doctors for the price of one. He didn't see it that way, however. He was too nervous to see the lab coat as half full. Only one doctor was the real doctor in his eyes. The other two were students, indentured decoration, fawning young females playing at practicing.

"Have you always had a lack of hair that far up your legs?" asked Dr. Mendelson.

"In general, I've never been very hirsute," answered Larry. *Did I just use the word hirsute?* he asked himself. "I remember when my ankles were taped for basketball back in high school it never bothered me. Some of the other guys on the team would scream when it was ripped off." *I am rambling*, he thought.

"And you say you first noticed the change in gait how long ago?" he asked.

Larry answered in wordy fashion, aware he was not helping very much. He felt himself a poor historian. He kept talking and apologizing as the doctor whispered to his yes-girls who didn't look old enough to order a drink, let alone medication.

Dr. Mendelson finally nodded and cleared his throat cutting off Larry mid-sentence and said to the others, "Yes, you're right. Attempting to find an Achilles reflex would be pointless. Right, enough is enough. We should get you to the lab for EMG and NCV testing." The humorless toadies nodded in agreement. "We could fit you in right now, if you want."

Larry reiterated his wish not to become a professional pin-cushion or a test-case patient. Either they could fix him or they couldn't. The doctor, the real one, assured him that the tests were necessary to make an accurate diagnosis.

"I'm supposed to be back at work this afternoon," said Larry. "How long will it take?"

"Oh, it'll only take forty-five minutes or so."

"Okay," agreed Larry. "You're the doctor. Let's do it."

"You'll be in good hands," said Dr. Mendelson handing Larry a prescription for orthotics. "Here, this should help your balance and allow you to walk better. We wouldn't be doing our jobs if you didn't improve. Good-bye."

Without waiting for a response the doctor turned and left. Larry realized the flunkies were now in charge and he scrambled to follow them down the hallway. They seemed unaware that it was difficult for him to keep up.

That was the last time Larry saw Dr. Mendelson.

"Ouch," said Larry. "We've been at this for over an hour and a half, you know. Dr. Mendelson said it would only take forty-five minutes."

"Sometimes it takes longer," said the tan one.

Yeah, when you don't know what you're doing, thought Larry. He was in too much pain to appreciate his own humor. For more than ninety minutes he'd been wired to electrodes. Sometimes the electrodes were armed with needles and were thrust deep into his muscles, again and again. He was told alternately to flex or rest muscle after muscle.

"I know it's difficult, but it won't work if you move. We need you to be still," said the short one.

I am being still, thought Larry. I know when I'm moving or not. I'm being still.

At one point the 'doctors' had to call in a technical specialist because they were having trouble finding something or other near Larry's left ankle. His feet are cold, he heard one of them say. Sometimes the pulses of electricity grew so intense they hurt more than the stabs and twists of the needles. I will never do this again, he thought. I'd rather limp for the rest of my life.

By the time they were finished he was down to one 'doctor'. The short one had been called away. Lunch probably, thought Larry. The tan one turned off the EMG and they started the walk back to the office. Larry asked her what she could see from the tests. But she wouldn't divulge anything.

"We won't know for certain until we go over all

the numbers and look at all the data," she said.

Larry knew that she was either lying or incompetent.

"Could you at least tell if there was demyelination or not?" he prodded.

"I really can't say until we've analyzed the results," she lied.

Suddenly she stopped. "Oh crap. Come on, we have to go back."

"Why?" asked Larry a little frightened they'd hurt him again.

"Nothing. We just have to go back."

Back in the lab Larry stood to the side and overheard the 'doctor' tell the tech that she'd turned off the machine before she'd printed out and forwarded the results. She begged him to recover the data. With the weary press of a button he restored the results. She hugged the tech and bounded down the hall again not waiting for her pained and limping patient.

The telephone display read Northwestern Hospital. He flushed with fear. Who was hurt? he thought. His wife? His mother? One of the children? A call from a hospital is never good news.

"This is Larry."

"Hello Mr. Derrida, this is Charles Hoagland from Dr. Mendelson's office, how are you?" said the telephone.

You should know how I am, thought Larry with momentary relief. "I'm well, thank you," he answered instead. This is the call he'd been waiting for. This is the call he'd been dreading. He braced himself for the worst.

"The doctor would like to see you again in two months, if you wouldn't mind?"

"Why?" asked Larry.

"Um, I don't understand," he replied.

"Why does he want to see me in two months?" repeated Larry.

"Well I am sure that's between you and the doctor," he said. "I was asked to schedule the appointment, that's all."

Two weeks of sleepless angst became angry disbelief. No, it was more than that, an entire decade of speculation, fear and hope surfaced too, and boiled over, a cauldron of frothy frustration. Their response to his problem, their grand learned reply, was another appointment. His reward for trusting them, for enduring their horrible tests, was deferral. He had agreed to play along for answers, any kind of answer, some explanation, but they had none.

Larry took a deep breath and cleared his throat.

"I understand that you are just doing your job. I get that. But indulge me, please. Two weeks ago I met with the doctor for the first time and was quite clear about my history, my hopes and my fears. I expressly told him that I was not interested in becoming a professional patient. He said he understood and casually suggested I immediately undergo two routine and, I might add, very painful tests to confirm his suspicions which he would not disclose until the tests were performed. And now the first contact I have with his office is a request to meet again two months from now. No diagnosis, no feedback, no discussion, nothing. So my question remains. For what purpose does he wish to see me?"

"I am sorry, Mr. Derrida, but I thought you'd already talked with the doctor after your test results. My only instructions here are to schedule an appointment at two months. I'm sorry."

"Mr. Hoagland, is it? I am sure you can appreciate that I'm at work and cannot really speak as freely as I'd like. Still, unless you can tell me anything more I am going to have to decline your invitation," said Larry.

"It says here neuropathy," said Hoagland audibly flustered but hopeful.

"We both know that's meaningless. I knew that before I saw him. I didn't need the tests to tell me that," barked Larry.

"Mr. Derrida, let me talk to the doctor. I'm not prepared to . . . I'll tell him what you've said and pass along your questions and your frustration. And I'll find out why the need for the two month appointment. Would that help?"

"Thank you," answered Larry.

Two days later Northwestern Hospital again flashed on Larry's work phone. This time it was expected.

"This is Larry."

"Hello Mr. Derrida, it's Charles from Northwestern, Dr. Mendelson's office, following-up as promised."

Larry did not reply.

"Well, good news, I spoke with the doctor and he said it would be okay if you met in six months instead of two. How's that?"

Larry ignored this burying of the lede and asked pointedly, "Did you get a diagnosis?"

"The doctor said it was a neuronapathy or axonopathy, most likely hereditary."

Larry whispered, "That still doesn't say much. He didn't give you a name? Is it ALS?" Years of internet research belched forth. "Was there demyelination? Are the axons compromised? Are the horn cells involved? Why no MRI? Did you talk about the prognosis? Will it get better or will it get worse?"

"I'm sorry, Mr. Derrida, that's all I was told. I'm sure at the six month appointment the doctor will be able to answer all your questions."

"There will not be a six month appointment," said Larry abruptly. "If that's all you are able to tell me I don't see any need to meet again."

"Of course that's up to you," said Hoagland, "but would it be okay if I asked the doctor to give you a call? Maybe he can say something to change your mind."

"That would be fine," said Larry. "Mr. Hoagland . . . Charles . . . you understand this has nothing to do with you, don't you? I'm terribly frustrated, that's all. I thought the tests, the doctors . . . I thought it would help. It didn't. I am looking for answers. And maybe there are none. It's been a long time. I'd like to be better."

"I understand, Mr. Derrida. I'll have the doctor give you a call. I am sorry I couldn't be more help. Good-bye."

"Good-bye. And thank you."

Dr. Mendelson never called. There was no second appointment.

Larry Derrida died because of his disease.

Kathleen knew that Larry's disturbing story about Dr. Mendelson's office was one-sided. She also knew that Larry tended to exaggerate and was prone to play the martyr. If even part of what he said is true though, she thought, it is totally unacceptable. As a healthcare provider and a wife she was doubly indignant.

A former patient (fifty-five year-old female, spiral fractures of the right tibia and right fibula—skiing accident) of Kathleen's was a doctor at Northwestern. Due to NOC's proximity to the hospital many of her patients were doctors. They were the worst patients, she'd often say. This particular patient, however, had the decency of being both a good patient and a well-respected neurologist. Kathleen asked her to contact Dr. Mendelson, maybe get a look at the test results, and let her know her opinion. In effect she asked for a backdoor second opinion. Medical professionals often help each other out, she explained to Larry. But the results were the same.

"They don't know," she said flatly.

"They don't have any idea? I find it difficult to believe that they don't have at least a suspicion. You can't tell me they don't have a guess. I know doctors and their egos are bigger than that."

Kathleen was quiet.

"You know something, don't you?"

"They really don't know, Larry. It's not like there's a definitive test for these things. It's more complicated than that. Neuro can be tricky."

"Tell me."

"Okay. But, remember, these diagnoses can be terribly difficult. They both think it's probably something like progressive muscular atrophy or primary lateral sclerosis, something in that family."

Larry was quiet.

"That family . . . that family is the ALS family."

"I know. I . . . I don't know what to say," said Kathleen trying not to tremble.

"Lou Gehrig's Disease. They think I have Lou Gehrig's Disease?"

"They really don't know. A lot of these things mirror other things. It takes a long time, years sometimes, to accurately diagnose certain neurological issues."

"Fucking ALS! You've got to be kidding me. I'll be damned."

Owen and Declan cried from the other room. Their parents cried too.

SIX

May the roof over your heads be as well thatched
as those inside are well matched.

If nothing else the Dolans were prolific. Kathleen's grandfather was one of nineteen children to plash through the puddles and dart across the country lanes of County Kilkenny. Her mother Mary, however, came from more restrained McNally stock and was able to limit her output to three. Kathleen herself had always wanted five children, a modest number for the twenty-first century, she thought. The birth of her third, a girl they named Sophia, changed her mind.

Three children in just over six years had made forty year-old Kathleen a relative stranger to herself. Her mind and her body had become almost unrecognizable, foreign. Where was the woman, a Trinity College graduate, mind you, who left the green isle of Ireland for the excitement, adventure and green currency of the United States? Where was the belly-pierced rebel who bungeed off a bridge in Australia and rafted down the Zambezi? What happened to the woman who dove the waters off the Galapagos Islands and trekked up to Machu Picchu? Youth, that capricious culprit, took these adventures away when it left. But what about her plans for graduate school?

What about law school? What about a career? And surely she would travel again. She had seen so little of the world really.

Her chestnut hair was cut short, a strand or two of gray lurked in the thickness. Her once taut belly jiggled beneath stretch marks. There were circles under her eyes that concealer could no longer hide. She felt as if she hadn't had a decent night's sleep in years. Life, Larry and children had changed her. It was evident in her mirror and in her routine. Dirty diapers displaced scuba gear, car seats displaced bungee cords, strollers displaced parachutes, and playdates displaced travel. It was surreal. It was like winning and losing combined. Not like tying, one didn't offset the other, nor was it as discrete. It was more like a process. It was fluid. It was like she'd donned a full body costume of domesticity that somehow fused over the woman, the girl, she'd been. But at the same time it was incongruously satisfying, fulfilling. She was more than she had been. She was still attractive for her age. She was still the woman from all those trips and experiences. It was all still there. Only now she was also a mother and a wife. It was different. And oddly that was enough. It was more than enough, she thought. She was happy. Not the happiness she had expected, but happiness nonetheless.

Larry Derrida died because of Kathleen.

The diagnosis or lack thereof tested her relative contentment. She couldn't help but blame him a little. It wasn't rational. It was anger. With objective certainty, the kind only mothers possess, she felt the weight of responsibility for her three small children and her sanity as she prepared to watch her husband waste away from a horrific, incurable disease. Like a fourth child. Some day. But then, once the initial shock had passed, Larry seemed better than before, more cheerful. The orthotics, the AFOs, helped him immensely. There was literally a spring back in his step thanks to the semi-flexible, white L-shaped pieces of molded plastic. He called them his new legs or sometimes just his legs. "Be there in a sec, I have to put on my legs." The limp disappeared. His confidence increased. But he refused to discuss the issue any further.

"It's pointless. I mean, what's the point? They couldn't do anything anyway. Let's just pretend we still don't know anything. I can walk better. I can play with the kids. That's enough. Let's forget it for now. Okay?"

"But what if there is something we can do, something we should be doing?" countered Kathleen.

"Tell you what, if you find something that I should be doing, a new possibility, a treatment, you let me know and I'll consider it. Until then we don't discuss it. Deal?"

And just like that she was supposed to forget it, to let it go.

The only time she was even partially successful letting it go was at work. She started to daydream that she worked more than twice a week. It would be too much for Larry's mother though, she thought. Her septuagenarian in-law, Jackie, was already run ragged caring for the brood every Tuesday and Thursday. Kathleen felt guilty enough watching grandma wave good-bye weakly to the children as she climbed into a cab after her long day of diapers and drama. They couldn't ask her to do more.

"I had my final follow-up with Roger the cop. He's back at work checking those badges. I don't know what you did, but he couldn't say enough about you," said Dr. Archer.

"Roger's a nice man. And a good patient," replied Kathleen.

"And you are a very good therapist. I just wanted to say thanks." He looked around. They were alone in the hallway. "You know if I have anything to say about it, you'll always have a job here," he whispered.

"Thank you," she said, flattered but wary.

He moved a little closer. "There's talk . . . there are rumors, what with Obamacare and so on, that we may have to sell NOC . . . that things are going to change." He edged even closer. "Between you and me it's more than rumor. Now I don't know exactly what the outcome will be. No one knows . . . precisely . . . yet. But the endgame's begun. I just wanted you to know so you could be prepared, that's all."

"Thank you . . . again," said Kathleen in a low voice.

There's nothing so bad that it can't be worse, thought Kathleen. She shook her head and chuckled to herself. There was no misunderstanding. She knew him well enough by now. The new owners, whoever they might be, are going to clean house. They would all be let go. She didn't know where to begin. Be prepared? She hadn't updated her résumé in fourteen years.

"You have an eval waiting in two," chirped a young assistant.

"Ah, thanks," she said taking the chart.

Kathleen pushed open the door and greeted her new patient with a caring, single-minded, welcoming smile, her problems, for the moment, forgotten.

SEVEN

Many a sudden change takes place on an unlikely day.

"Are we really going to do this?"

"Movement, any kind of movement, is, by definition, a physical process. It's all about inertia. An avalanche in the Alps, the ever-shifting sands of the Sahara, the Ping-Pong balls picked in the lottery and the evacuation of your bowels are all types of movement. The physical antecedents and forces are clear in each case. But what about ideas? Can ideas move objects? Is an idea physical? Scientists think they originate, like consciousness, in our brains, our *physical* brains. Does that make an idea physical or something else? Do ideas really change the world? Can ideas move, physically move, people? What does it take to move an entire family? Does it require some kind of social inertia, some magical combination of perceived external forces and provocative ideas? Perhaps it's all just semantics.

For years Larry and Kathleen had talked of moving to Europe. Though they shared a love of travel, the discussions weren't serious. They were *viva voce* dreams of escape and adventure, the kind of talk two middle-aged married people have late at night after a bottle or two of wine. The 'what would you do with your lotto winnings' kind of talk. Invariably the talk of moving abroad smashed into the reality of their three young children and their one modest bank balance. If only I were independently wealthy, dreamt Larry.

In 2011 Larry wasn't the only one wishing for more money. The country was still mired in the middle of its long recession. The unemployment rate was in double digits. Two of his immediate neighbors had lost their homes to foreclosure. He watched his own home, the cute yellow Victorian with the green lawn, lose more value every day. And it wasn't just Chicago, or the United States. The world was in trouble. Irish banks were bought by the government. Greece begged for handout after handout. Masses protested. Cities declared bankruptcy. People everywhere suffered.

Larry Derrida died because the world had changed.

Five year-old Owen didn't know people suffered; nor did he know his dad was dying. His world was much smaller and safer, filled with playgrounds and Pokémon. After a year of pre-school he had tested into one of the elite public elementary schools in the city: a classical school miles away from their home, but worth the commute. Larry and Kathleen were thrilled for and proud of their eldest child. Owen thrived. He loved the school. His parents, however, had to consider the probability that Owen's siblings, when the time came, might not test into the same school. Three separate schools every morning and every afternoon would put a lot of wear and tear on the BMW and the family.

At first, when Kathleen told Larry that she might lose her job, he was inwardly pleased. He had always wanted to be the sole breadwinner of the family. It was egotism wrapped in testosterone. He found the idea of his wife at home taking care of the domestic duties a throwback to a simpler, more authentic, time. He questioned the misogynous feeling, but never answered the question. Stay-at-home Kathleen also came with the bonus that his mother could be a grandmother rather than a babysitter.

"I could always find another job," said Kathleen, "probably not at the same pay or the same hours. But I'll be able to get another job."

"We'll worry about that if it happens," said Larry. "You said yourself it's just a rumor at this point. Maybe it'll all fall through. You never know. And you know it's not about the money."

"Maybe. The money helps. Anyway, I just want you to know that I will be able to find work though, if I—we—want," she said. "That you don't have to worry." There was a part of Kathleen that really didn't want to look for another job. Part of her, a big part, wanted to quit working entirely and stay home with the kids. She wanted them to be a family while there was still time. She didn't share this with Larry.

"We'll see," said Larry. "We can cross that bridge when we come to it, I suppose."

There are moments in life when wishes come true. Kathleen lost her job and Larry received a raise. Their unspoken hopes were satisfied. There are also moments in life when you wish your wishes hadn't come true. This was one of those times for the Derridas.

"It means they like your work, right? That's a good thing. That's why they gave you more money. That's how it usually works, isn't it?" asked Kathleen teasingly.

"Seems so," said Larry.

"So what's the problem?" she asked.

"The whole thing is the problem. That's the problem. Work is the problem," fired Larry. "You don't understand. You couldn't." He took a deep breath before continuing. "Yes, it's more money. And that's great. That's fine. But the job . . . what I do . . . what I did . . . is done. The entire landscape has changed. After fourteen years I feel like the new kid on the block . . . like I'm being made to justify my position. It's ridiculous. I feel . . . I feel naked, if that makes any sense. The whole thing is ludicrous. It's insane. I no longer report to Jay for one. Now he'll probably retire so I can't even go to him for advice. Almost my entire team has been laid off, that's two. I hate BHI. It's poisonous. And, three, my position is now dependent, get this, on stories—creating stories.

There's the problem . . . problems . . . for you. Any more questions?"

Kathleen waited for Larry to calm down before she answered. "Of course I have questions. But first, you knew Jay wasn't going to be around forever. That's life. You knew that. It's awful that your team was let go, but times are tough. You should feel good that they kept you on. Also, and most significantly, companies don't give more money to people they're trying to get rid of. Now that would be ridiculous. And, you're right, I can't fully understand what it all means. I have no idea what you're talking about when you say you now have to tell stories. I don't know what that means. But I do know that you can do whatever you set your mind to. I do know the man that I married. I do know that you'll be a success. I have faith in you. That I know. "

"Sorry, I shouldn't unload on you. It's not you. It's just a lot to process. It's all so new and raw," said Larry.

"It's okay. It's what I signed up for," smiled Kathleen weakly.

Larry explained the details of his new position to his wife. The BHI questions had all been asked. The behemoth had done the calculations and spit out the data. The big data was theirs. Bytes upon bytes of the stuff. It was his new job to take these bytes and monetize them. It was his new job to make the big data financially meaningful by creating narratives, stories and concepts, to tie to proposed marketing plans. It was his new job to use their big data to tell the stories that sell health insurance products. His new job, then, was to take the most intimate, albeit anonymous, information about millions of people and use it against them. To analyze their vulnerabilities and exploit them. He had become a hustler, a shill for insurance. He had become an insurance salesman. Maybe he had been one ever since he'd started with BCBS. But now, for the first time, he felt like one.

"Let's just forget the ick factor for the time being, okay?" said Larry. "That I can get past. I'm an adult, I've already compromised myself to the point of not caring. The thing is that I'm afraid. I'm scared I won't be able to do it. I don't know anything about advertising. I'm afraid I'll fail. And if I fail, we are done. We won't be able to make the mortgage payment, the car payment. And what if I get sick? We're toast. It's scary."

"Relax. I'm sure they wouldn't have given you the job if they didn't think you could do it. Don't think of it as advertising, think of it just like you said, think of it as telling stories."

"Tell stories. What if I can't?"

"You've got a Masters in literature and you don't think you can tell a story," laughed Kathleen. "Are you serious?" He's afraid of success, she thought.

"I prefer the lyric. Give me poetry over prose any day. Besides, pure invention is but the talent of a liar."

"That is not you talking. It's one of your poets," mocked Kathleen gently.

"Difficult to imagine Byron peddling insurance," answered Larry.

Larry Derrida died because he was afraid.

And he was right. Larry could not tell a story. He worked harder than ever. He saw Kathleen and the kids only on Sunday mornings. He tried. He repurposed plots from novels and episodes from *I Love Lucy*. He reread all of Henry James. Everything was rejected. He could not tell a story. He did not tell his wife. He pretended everything was going well. He told her his initial fears were, as she predicted, unjustified. He lied . . . to protect her.

When the tips of his fingers began to tingle Larry knew it was time to confess. He assumed the stress, the combined strain of failing and of hiding his failure, was exacerbating his illness. He felt something bad was going to happen and felt he owed it to Kathleen and the children to warn them.

Following a late Wednesday night dinner and a customary bottle of red table wine, the kids tucked into bed, little Declan and his over-sized tonsils snoring loudly upstairs, Larry blurted out the truth. Part of the truth, anyway.

"You know I'll never find a job that pays as well as this one."

"What are you talking about?" asked Kathleen. "Who says you have to find another job?"

"It's not going well. I haven't been completely

honest with you lately. I'm sorry. It hasn't been going well at all. There is talk, speculation," he answered. "I told you I couldn't tell a goddamned story."

"I'm sure you're exaggerating. And imagining. Any new job takes time. They know that. You'll get it. I'm sure. Maybe you're just trying too hard. Maybe that's the problem."

"That's not the problem," he said. "The problem is that I've been in over my head for years. I've never belonged there. The truth is that I've known this day was coming for more than a decade."

"What do you want to do?"

"I don't know. Leave? Quit?"

"You know if you want to quit you can. I'm on your side. You don't have to be at a job you hate. Quit if you are miserable, but don't quit because you think you'll be fired. Let them fire you. Though for the record I think you are wrong," she said.

Larry knew she would say this.

"Here's my thought," he began. "Hear me out. If I wait until they let me go—which they will, despite your confidence—we'll be trapped financially. Just to keep the house we'll have to eat into our savings. And we both know if I get a job the pay will be half of what I'm making now. I'm not even qualified to be doing the job I have. Sure, you could go to work fulltime and that would help, but it would put a big burden on my mom to take care of the kids and we would still struggle to pay for the car and the house, a house which isn't even worth what we paid for it. At some point we'd have to sell the house for a loss after going through everything we've worked to save. The alternative would be to walk away from the house altogether. Either way we would lose our biggest investment along with most of our savings."

"Pretty bleak picture," said Kathleen.

"I agree. And maybe it is a worst case scenario. Still it's awful to even contemplate. But, listen, what if I quit first rather than waiting to be fired? That would give us some control over things, wouldn't it? We could sell the house sooner, get our finances in order. That kind of stuff. Be proactive. Take charge of the situation. We'd be moving from a position of strength, not desperation."

"Move?"

"Where?"

"I don't know. We've talked about Europe forever. It's always been Spain or France. Why not? Let's do it. You could be closer to your family. Wouldn't that be nice? It won't get any easier later. If not now, when? I'll be fifty before you know it. And the kids, especially Owen, in another year or two they'll be too old to go. It wouldn't be fair to them when they have their friends and schools."

"Okay, let's say I'm in. Is it Spain or France?" she asked.

"If we're really going to do this," said Larry, "I'd vote for France. Spain is cheaper and I'd love the kids to learn Spanish. But France has something."

"A *je ne sais quoi?*"

"Yes, that's it, a *je ne sais quoi*."

"My vote is for France too," said Kathleen. "And if we're going to do this we're going to do it right. Agreed?"

"Of course," answered Larry.

"Isn't this crazy?"

They opened another bottle of wine to celebrate the decision. Plans flowed.

"We don't do anything, say anything, until the house is sold," demanded Kathleen.

"We should wait until the spring if possible. We could use my bonus," said Larry.

"Do we ship our furniture? What about the car?"

"What will our friends think?"

"I can't believe we are really going to do this."

"Do you think the kids will have any problems learning the language?"

"France is a big place. Where in France?"

"What will we do for work?"

"I promise we won't go hungry. I'll do whatever it takes."

"We should start on the language right away. I haven't had any French since college."

"How much money do you think we have? Enough for a year or two?"

"I'm sure they need PTs in France," said Larry.

"And I'm positive you'd be able to get a job teaching English if you wanted," proffered Kathleen.

"It'll be a different lifestyle."

"Downsizing."

"We don't need all these *things*."
"We'll be able to travel all over Europe!"
"Our children will be fluent in French."
"The food . . . the wine . . . the culture."
"What will your mother think?"

Upstairs Sophia rolled over in her crib and sighed.

In the final analysis we are all closet misoneists. And yet we choose change all the time.

"Are we really going to do this?"

EIGHT

It is not with the first stroke that a tree falls.

A shared hangover didn't temper enthusiasm for the move. They decided springtime in France had a nice, if clichéd, ring to it. Assuming Larry kept his job they would have a last five figure bonus to add to the coffers, plus it gave them plenty of time to take care of the preparations. April in Paris, a perfect prospect. But pragmatism possesses its own power.

"If we wait until next year to put the house on the market, what are the odds it will sell by the time we want to leave? In this climate I would say zero, wouldn't you?" asked Larry.

"I agree. So do we put it up for sale now?" responded Kathleen.

"I think that's the smart thing to do, don't you?"

They had an offer on the house three days after it was listed on the MLS.

The best laid schemes o' Mice an' Man/Gang aft agley,/An' len'e us nought but grief an' pain,/For promis'd joy!

I knew we should have priced it higher, thought

Larry. Their realtor was a friend of Kathleen's. Real estate agents are bloated ticks sucking on the shriveled skin of a dying industry. "They are beneath worthless," said Larry.

They had six weeks to closing, a month and a half until homelessness. Their original nine-month timetable for research, preparations, packing, and goodbyes vanished with the stroke of a pen. The new compressed plan put the family on a plane in late October.

Before they could book their flight there was much to do.

The first thing they did was count the money. After adding the estimated proceeds from the house sale, selling their furniture and car, divesting their stocks, and cashing in their savings and checking accounts, the total came to $185,500. They also each had about $125,000 in 401(k) money that they hoped they would not have to plunder.

    On the other side of the ledger they figured that they'd have around $10,000 in expenses before they left: plane tickets, movers, incidentals, etc.

    One hundred and seventy-five thousand dollars for a family of five put Paris and the south of France safely out of reach. Rather quickly they decided on Bretagne, or Brittany as it's known in English, as their new European home. It was relatively close to Ireland and Kathleen's family, an hour by plane; and Larry, who disliked flying, could even take an overnight ferry if he wished. The region was known for good schools and for being friendly and welcoming. Housing prices were among the best in France. There was also a sizeable contingent of English speakers which Larry and Kathleen thought might make the transition a little easier. Neither one of them had ever spent any time in Brittany, yet, sight unseen, Brittany it was.

Larry looked for a rental property in the middle of Brittany.

Kathleen researched moving and shipping companies.

They bought Rosetta Stone and started to learn French.

The lawyers and realtors called with questions and concerns.

They told their family and then their friends about their momentous decision.

Their family and friends were shocked.

Larry's mother cried.

Kathleen began packing.

They explained the move to the children. Owen cried. He cried because he would miss his school and his friends. Declan cried because Owen cried and because he would miss his neighbors and his yellow house and green backyard. Sophia saw everyone upset and cried too.

Larry waited to give notice at work . . . just in case the sale of the house fell through at the last minute.

They set up online bill pay for all their credit cards.

Larry paid $1,500 for a back-up set of legs. He was tempted to get them in black this time but stayed with white.

Kathleen visited the French consulate for advice and any paperwork they might need. She learned that their Illinois driver's licenses could be easily exchanged for French ones.

Larry contacted an estate agent who agreed to sell their belongings and haul away everything that didn't sell. The catch was that they had to move out of the house before the sale.

They culled years of accumulated paperwork and sorted passports, inoculation records, tax returns and insurance policies.

Kathleen informed Owen's school about his departure.

Larry no longer noticed the tingling in his hands.

Kathleen made doctors' appointments for everyone.

Larry had a cavity filled by his dentist. She mentioned

he could use some work on his gums and he said he was moving to France.

Kathleen put her Illinois physical therapist's license on inactive and cancelled her malpractice insurance.

They both brutally discarded possessions and letters they'd been hauling around for decades.

They met with bankers to make sure it would be easy to access their money from Brittany.

Larry had to repaint the basement storm doors. It was one of the conditions the VA mandated to approve the buyers' loan.

They burned all their music to their new laptop and gave away their CDs.

Owen promised several of his classmates and friends that he would be a good pen pal from France.

Kathleen submitted a change of address at the post office.

Neither one of them slept well.

Jacqueline, Larry's mother, the children's grandmother, visited every day. And cried. Every day.

Kathleen put an ad on Craigslist to sell the BMW.

Larry found a three bedroom rental house in a tiny village in central Brittany for 550 euros per month plus utilities. Their lease was to begin on the first of November.

Kathleen debated having surgery on her varicose veins. She decided it could wait.

Some nights they were excited, others they were panic-stricken. Sometimes both during the same night.

Kathleen had a fight with her best friend. Her friend felt abandoned. So did Kathleen.

Larry went to see Dr. Youklis for a check-up and asked for a large supply of diazepam so he could fly free of fear for many years to come.

Kathleen packed.

Larry came up with an idea for work, a consulting idea. He could sell his ideas to BCBS from France on a per story basis. They only paid if they bought the story.

Evenings were filled. They had drinks and dinners with friends. Every toast was tearful.

Knowing the end was near, Larry's work became more agreeable.

Kathleen changed their online contact information.

Larry put in his notice and pitched his consulting idea.

Kathleen packed and purged.

Kathleen taught the kids a few words of French and showed them pictures of the Eiffel Tower.

Larry cut the green grass for the last time.

They sold their car to CarMax.

Larry purchased five round-trip (much cheaper than one-way) tickets to Paris on American Airlines leaving on the twenty-seventh of October.

They asked their landlord if they could get into the house a few days before the lease began. They were told for an extra one hundred euros it would be possible.

Due to the estate sale and closing date the Derridas had to stay in Jacqueline's one bedroom apartment for the final two weeks before the flight. Larry joked that it would make the transition to the wilds of Brittany a little easier on them all. The change and the discomfort might make the move a tad more palatable, he contended. He put on a brave face.

They were overwrought.

Larry wept on his last day at the office. Stress no doubt.

They were convinced they'd forgotten things.

The Taylors from next door presented the Derridas

with a scrapbook of photos chronicling five years of the two families celebrating holidays, playing together and being good neighbors. Tears welled. Kathleen packed the gift with their important papers.

They ordered a taxi van for the airport.

Larry Derrida died because of a mistake.

NINE

A drink precedes a story.

The pills worked.

Not that Larry slept while the aircraft hurtled through the clouds defying common sense. No, the pills worked to the extent that he was not a white-knuckled, jaw-clenched mess, a bundle of exposed, quivering nerves, unable to do anything but stare straight ahead and imagine the plane dropping out of the sky amid screams and panic, warning bells and horror, the unspeakable darkness of the end. The little oval tablets did not, however, knock him out, make him unable to function, render him incapable of assisting with the children who, each in their individual way, struggled to behave in the unnatural environment of commercial transoceanic flight. Larry had to experiment to achieve his relative success; it was trial and error, or rather persistence, that finally won the day. His doctor had suggested one tablet of two milligrams half an hour before boarding and another should that not prove enough, but Larry, ever suspicious of medications, thought it prudent to consult the pharmacist who advised him to take half a pill one hour before boarding and gauge its effectiveness.

In this disparity of competing philosophies and expert opinions, Larry was pressed to design his own dosage regimen which eventuated in the ingestion of a total of six milligrams, three white pills, swallowed with aid of water over the span of an hour and a half, followed by two large, as large as air travel will allow, glasses of red wine swilled in great haste approximately one hour after take-off. While the potentially unsafe combination of diazepam and alcohol did not make Larry's flight enjoyable, it did to a great extent blunt the expectation and unpleasantness of imminent death.

Declan, of them all, was most bothered by the intermittent turbulence. There are few things more pathetic than a child who is trying to behave but just cannot. It's like watching a two-legged dog try to walk. Overtired and unable to sleep in the rocking airship, Declan tossed and turned and moaned and cried for almost eight straight hours, his mother unable to comfort him despite the pitiable imploring of his big, brown, bloodshot eyes.

Owen sat across the aisle from the rest of the family. The plan had been to switch seats once the plane was in the air so he would not have to be by himself for the entire flight. Almost immediately he struck up a conversation with the man next to him, asking about his Hasidic dress. After satisfying his curiosity—which took an hour and a half—he read a chapter of *Harry Potter*, ate his entire meal and drifted off to sleep waking just as breakfast was being served.

Sophia blathered nonstop for the first hour they were on the plane asking questions about everyone and everything. This was her first time on an airplane and she felt the urgent need to tell each and every passenger of her special status. But the novelty wore off, the hour grew late and, after Kathleen managed to get her to eat a portion of pasta, Sophia snuggled up against her mother's free arm and fell asleep.

Kathleen neither ate nor slept on American Airlines flight forty-two from Chicago to Paris.

Kathleen's ministering to the children, eight hours of comforting whispers, blanket tucks and bathroom runs, prevented her from enjoying the flight to their new home. Unlike her husband, she loved air travel: sailing slowly, seemingly, high above cottony clouds beyond the burden of gravity, gazing hour after hour upon hypnotic white-capped waves or trying to decipher an ever-changing patchwork of land- and cityscape; but most of all she enjoyed talking to strangers on a plane, strangers with fascinating back-stories on their way to or coming from exotic locales; these conversations brought back the excitement of her youthful travels and reminded her that the world was still an interesting, big place and there were adventures awaiting. There were to be no such conversations on this trip what with Larry seated in a different row, Declan moaning in her lap and a sleeping Sophia leaning precariously against her leg. There were moments, however few, for her to escape with her thoughts. She tried to picture their new lives in France but the variables proved too many and she turned her mind to her husband. Flying had never been his favorite thing to do and now with his legs it became even more stressful. She replayed the image of him at airport security as he calmly informed the uniformed TSA agents that he could not remove his shoes because of a medical condition. She reflected on how gallant he looked undergoing the humiliation of a comprehensive security check as his children watched. She felt for him and did her best to take his condition into account in every instance. She did everything she could think of to make his life easier. She watched his head bob as he tried to sleep and smiled thinking that sometimes she did make his life easier.

A fat man walking to the WC lost his balance and bumped against Sophia momentarily waking her up.

Larry's hands were not sweating and he took this as a sign he might be able to sleep a bit. He turned to make sure Kathleen and the kids were comfortable. She smiled while adjusting a pillow for Sophia. They all seem to be doing quite well all things considered, he thought as he closed his eyes. His mind turned to the future. A kaleidoscope of life in France flashed before his semi-consciousness: it was a vision of a pristine stone villa with a black tiled roof reflecting the noonday sun overlooking a clear, glittering stream in the valley below; Larry sits in the shaded slated courtyard sipping wine and eating from a warm baguette spread with cheese from their neighbors' farm, a well-thumbed Oxford Authors compilation of Byron's poetry rests open on the stone table; Kathleen lowers her glass from her lips and laughs at the children playing among the fruit trees screaming with delight in pitch-perfect French; Larry rises from his chair and kisses his wife on the forehead; Kathleen asks where he's going; Larry points to the fully renovated cottage they use for an office and says, I've got to create more stories; Kathleen tells him to stay and enjoy the day, you've already sold so many, and it's made us so much money, please, take the day off, relax; Larry laughs in agreement, sits down and pours another glass of wine as the sun reaches its apogee, the slight breeze carries Edith Piaf's voice to his ears and Larry thinks to himself that if perfection exists it would be very close to this.

The Derridas were the very last passengers to deplane.

"I'll drive," said Larry.

"I don't think so," said Kathleen. "Read the label on your pills."

"But I'm fine."

"I'll drive, please," she stated, reaching for the car key.

They were both silently thankful that they had spent the additional $140 and rented a car with GPS. If nothing else it saved them at least forty minutes alone escaping the confines of Charles de Gaulle Airport. There was, however, an anxious moment when they entered the address of their destination and the electronic navigator informed them in a soothing female voice that no such residence could be found. For a split second Larry thought the rental might have been some kind of internet scam. He tried a second time and the machine responded.

The weather was fair, the car was nice, the road was smooth, the journey long. But the children slept, Larry commented on the changing scenery of each *department* and Kathleen kept them all on the right route to Lanrelas. Around noonish they pulled off into a tiny rest stop off the motorway to stretch their legs and use the toilets. They observed a French couple in their mid-thirties sitting at a picnic table eating lunch. They had spread out a checked tablecloth, porcelain plates, glinting flatware and even a full bottle of wine. It looked like they were prepared for a three hour meal. Larry commented quietly on the hazards of drinking and driving.

"I guess we're not in Kansas anymore," he laughed.

The drive took five and a half hours. Kathleen made it on adrenaline alone.

A few minutes before the sun dipped below the horizon, the GPS guided the Derrida's rented Peugeot to the front of their rented house in a tiny village amid rolling hills and whispering wind turbines.

They'd reached Lanrelas.

TEN

Be they kings, or poets, or farmers,
they're a people of great worth,
they keep company with the angels,
and bring a bit of heaven here to earth.

Larry and Kathleen both noticed the flies first. Mounds and mounds of dead flies stared at them through the windows. They tried to shield the gruesome sight from the children by allowing them to run around the backyard while they explored the house. The windows of death added tension to the turn of the key. But on the other side of the door it was just a house, a little musty perhaps, but just a house. The windows, though, were something else. Upstairs, more flies. Behind every shutter, against every pane of glass, mass after mass of lifeless flies awaited discovery. Kathleen set to work removing the corpses as Larry unloaded the car.

They lit candles to remove the odor vacancy had left behind.

The next morning, their first morning in Brittany, the flies were back. And, while flies may be able to tell the difference, Kathleen thought they looked exactly like the flies she'd disposed of the night before.

Apart from its location at the geographical center of Brittany, there isn't much to recommend Lanrelas. It does lie five miles southeast of some unspectacular gorges, which prove of middling interest to hikers and sightseers. Lanrelas looks, on its surface, like hundreds of other unremarkable villages scattered throughout the French northwest. It sits on a small rise overlooking a patchwork of farm fields and forests carved up by black ribbons of well-maintained roads leading to bigger places. No more than 400 souls, mostly farmers and retirees, call Lanrelas home.

The house came with instructions, an instruction booklet really, detailing the quirks of the building, the village and Brittany. It was a combination tourist brochure and guide to living in the house and Lanrelas: the town hosts two cafes, a *boulangerie*, a small grocery store, a post office, the mayor's office; the gorges—offering wonderful hiking—are quite close; be sure to check out the ossuary by the church; there is a swimming pool in Carhaix and a mini-golf course in Loudeac; the heating system requires heating oil—an expense not in the Derrida's budget—call Mr. Garandel to refill the tank; the range is powered by natural gas, you can purchase a new canister next to the post office; garbage and recyclables should be brought to the bins behind the mayor's office; to engage the lock on the backyard door turn the handle 90 degrees before inserting the key; and should you need anything or have additional questions do not hesitate to call upon Florence and Maxim down the street, they are good friends, speak a little English and run the only restaurant in Lanrelas, which, by the way, serves up very good and reasonably priced traditional dishes.

The day after they arrived in town Florence rapped on the door, introduced herself to the Derridas, and asked if they needed anything. She stayed and talked for an hour and a half. She could not have been kinder or more welcoming. Larry suspected she was being paid by their landlord.

Bretons are short, dark and ruddy as a rule. Brythonic Celts, half dust, half deity, thought Larry. They make up for their physiognomy by being perhaps the nicest people on the planet and any perceived lack of attractiveness is more than compensated by their intelligence, hard work and common sense. Simultaneously simple and interesting, they have the good fortune of possessing the favorable aspects of provincialism and cosmopolitanism in equal measure. Bretons farm and play the harp. They fish and quote poetry. They circle dance and vote socialist. They honor the dead and plan for the future. They teach Breton language and culture in their schools. They celebrate the present, ever conscious of the history pumping through their veins.

Larry Derrida died because he was born.

The Yellow Pages directory in France is ordered alphabetically by town first, according to specialty. So, in order to locate a business, any business, you must first know *where* you want to look. And, keep in mind, that Brittany is just slightly smaller than West Virginia. Now, while this might work well if you live in a large city with hundreds of choices, it does not work quite as well for those in tiny villages or hamlets, particularly if you are unfamiliar with the area. Lanrelas is near St. Nicholas which is near Rostrenen which is near Ploughnevel. Should you live in the environs of Lanrelas and find yourself in need of, say, an electrician, you must first look up Lanrelas electricians and, finding none, widen your search, town by alphabetical town, until you finally find someone to fix your fuse box. It takes a good map and a great deal of patience to find what you're searching for. It's like vendors are hiding from their customers in plain sight, almost like they do not want the business. On the other hand it presumably limits competition.

Approaching from the south Lanrelas forms an upside-down letter Y. There are tiny lanes shooting off the three main branches, but it is generally a three-street town of Breton-style granite-trimmed houses. The Salle des Fetes is the first public building in full view. A low-slung, blue-painted wood structure used for village dances, celebrations and formalities, it isn't much more than one large room with a bar and a kitchen. Across the street sits the *boulangerie* and Café Ciel. When the weather obliges, café customers perch on plastic chairs and gaze in remembrance upon the war memorial and the town's fifteenth century church, St. Gregory. Every town in Brittany has a church and every town has a war memorial. *Égalité*. All the war memorials in France appear to have been erected after World War I, and Lanrelas' is no exception. After World War II and the Algerian War, names and plaques were added to remember those who lost their lives. Year round fresh flowers surround the statue. Behind the memorial stands St. Gregory's Church, encircled by its cemetery and flanked by two religious statues, a Calvary (the original destroyed in the Revolution) and a Pietà. The church, largely rebuilt in the mid-nineteenth century is unremarkable though it does possess a rather interesting, if weathered, sixteenth century dragon finial over the south door. The real attraction—the one true tourist attraction in Lanrelas, though somewhat macabre—is one of the last remaining ossuaries with relics in Brittany and, for that matter, in all of France. Immediately to the left of the church gate, almost hidden by a pillar, is the small ossuary with its original fifteenth century columns. A peek inside reveals masses of neatly piled, gleaming white skulls, femurs, ulnas and other bones. Past the ossuary and the presbytery you get to the heart of the village, where the three main streets converge. Stuffed into the crotch of the roadway Y are the official buildings of the village: the post office, the mayor's office and the school. On one side of the school is a garbage/recycle area and on the other a rarely used tennis court with a splintered bench and sagging net. Across one leg of the Lanrelas Y is Florence's and Maxim's restaurant and across the other leg is the tiny grocery store.

Almost a decade earlier, when Larry quit smoking—

cold turkey—he had the strangest sensation for the first three or four days, like his body was being held back by invisible forces, like he was moving about in an unseen viscous gel. Everything he did seemed labored, muted and blurred. He assumed the feeling was the sensation of nicotine withdrawal. He experienced the same feeling the first few days in Lanrelas. Kathleen felt it too. They had gone cold turkey from everything they'd known and possessed in Chicago. They had shed their twenty-first century skin. No cell phones, no iPad, no telephone ringing, no sirens. It was strange.

They had thirteen days before they had to return the rental car. In order to buy a car of their own they had to first have a local bank account. Thanks to their real estate contact they found a banker who spoke English in the small town of Plemet. They opened an account and applied for a credit card, which was really nothing more than a debit card. They opened the account without a deposit and would be charged monthly for both the account and the card. This was normal in France they were told. The kids received bright balloons from the banker.

Their landlord had activated the telephone line but the Derridas were asked to purchase a phone on their arrival and they would be reimbursed. Larry bought the first one he saw. A Philips. They plugged it in and nothing happened. The user's manual for the telephone was written in twelve languages, including

Hungarian and Basque, but not English.

The Derridas drove around and around central Brittany (the rental car came with unlimited mileage) investigating houses for sale that Kathleen had found before they left Chicago. Again the GPS proved invaluable. Kathleen also befriended a second real estate agent who showed them additional properties that had just come on the market.

They followed the fluctuations of the dollar and the euro as much as they could. They whispered hopes that the euro would crash, strengthening the dollar and their purchasing power.

The flies kept returning. Larry called them Lazarus flies. They learned later that these flies that won't die are a well-known phenomenon throughout Brittany. The simple theory among the locals is that flies like farms.

Larry unknotted five separate wires and got the ancient analog television to work, all three and a half channels. Channel four only appeared when the mood struck. The kids were content to watch cartoons in French. One night Larry and Kathleen turned the set on and saw Bruce Jenner speaking French in a dubbed episode of *Keeping Up with the Kardashians*. They quickly changed the channel.

The nearest supermarket was the Super U in St. Nicholas. It was fifteen or twenty minutes away depending on whether or not a tractor slowed your trip. Kathleen learned to navigate the roads to and the aisles of the Super U. To unlock a cart you had to insert a euro into the small slot. She practiced her French reading the labels on food items. Super U carried everything from beer to bicycles, meat to motor oil. Wine and bread were dirt cheap, most other things were a little more expensive than the U.S. For some reason scissors were ridiculously cheap. The French must cut a lot, thought Kathleen.

The days between Halloween (October 31) and Remembrance Day (November 11) were, unbeknownst to the Derridas, a kind of unofficial holiday period in France where shops changed their business hours or closed altogether without rhyme or reason. Banks, supermarkets, the post and mayor's offices, even McDonald's, maintained wildly unpredictable hours despite ubiquitous signs declaring that they were open, *ouverte*.

Kathleen scrubbed the house from top to bottom, disinfecting everything in sight. Sometimes twice.

The day the Wi-Fi box arrived was like they'd won the lottery. And the installation guide came in English. Reconnected with the world, the iPad, email, even something as simple as reading the news made them feel like they'd returned to civilization. They skyped with Jacqueline who cried when she saw her faraway pixelated grandchildren.

Kathleen was excited when Florence told her that the restaurant was going to have a curry night and she could get take-away, *à emporter*. Kathleen arrived at the restaurant to pick up her order where they teased her, kindly of course, because she hadn't brought her own dishware for the pick-up. Maxim loaned her a couple of pots from the kitchen. Her cluelessness was the joke of the town for a month.

Larry used the internet to download an English instruction manual for the telephone.

Kathleen took the silver Opel mini-van for a test drive. Larry found driving a manual transmission with his armored legs much more difficult than he'd assumed. They'd found the car dealership in Pontivy because it was near the McDonald's and the children's palates were still dialed to U.S fast food. Larry talked to the salesman, François, who didn't try to sell at all. François excused himself to take cigarette breaks and chat with his colleagues. He honestly could not have cared a whit whether he made the sale or not. He spent more time tuning the showroom television to cartoons for the kids than trying to sell their parents a vehicle. It was an odd experience for Larry and Kathleen. Nonplussed, they bought the used Opel for 7,000 euros.

One evening a large truck from the port town of Le Havre pulled up in front of the house and unloaded two pallets, everything they had shipped by boat from the United States. There were thirty-seven boxes in all and miraculously everything arrived undamaged. Their clothing options expanded dramatically, they were reunited with their linen and they finally had a decent pizza-cutter and sharp knives.

In the beginning it rained a lot. It was also very windy. Because of this there were frequent power outages. Their neighbors came to the door to check on the Americans. Larry and Kathleen kept flashlights, matches and candles within easy reach. More than once they had to clear out the refrigerator and discard the thawed perishables.

The Bretons have a saying which loosely transliterated means, 'it only rains on the stupid'.

Number eight Rue des Ecoliers, the Derrida's house, was a typical neo-Breton, two-story building painted a pale yellow with granite stones exposed around the windows and door. On the ground floor was a kitchen with a creaking floor across from a living room with an out-of-service fireplace. Down the hall was a bathroom, a laundry room and a game room, which was cold and dusty. At the top of the elm staircase were three bedrooms of various sizes. One was hardly bigger than a closet. The bed pillows were flat and square and all the linen was embroidered. There was a small grass-covered backyard ringed by bushes with waxy leaves; an old tree stump awaiting removal sat in the corner. A few flat stones next to the back door pretended to be a patio.

Banks sell all kinds of insurance in France. In order to close the deal on the car Larry and Kathleen had to revisit their banker and obtain auto insurance. Like everyone they met she was beyond helpful explaining the pros and cons of each policy. She was forced to fudge a date on the paperwork when Larry informed her he'd been driving since he was sixteen years-old. In France no one can have a license before the age of eighteen. She also asked for proof they had previous insurance. The Derridas had never thought to keep copies of old car insurance policies since they'd be buying a new car and not transporting their old one. In France, explained the banker, the driver is insured and we must know what kind of driver you are and, unfortunately, here in France you have no record and thus must be treated as a new driver.

"Despite the fact that I've been driving for more than thirty years?" asked Larry.

"I'm afraid so. And this makes your payment much higher than it should be. See," she said showing them the monthly premium on her monitor.

"Yikes," said Kathleen. "That's more than double what we were paying for our BMW back home."

"Now, since you need the insurance immediately to purchase your car we can go ahead and process the policy, but if you could ask your old insurer for a letter, an attestation, that you have not made a claim we can adjust your rate to reflect your good American driving record," she suggested.

Once the bank received the letter from Allstate their monthly premium dropped by seventy percent and was adjusted retroactively. It's strange how it works, thought Larry, but it works.

Larry and Kathleen were thrilled when two neighbor boys knocked on the door and asked to play with Owen and Declan. Their first French friends, they thought. How darling! It turned out though that the boys only wanted access to the game room and the video game system so they could play games that they were not allowed to play at home. Kathleen walked in on them one afternoon as one of the boys was dismembering a zombie with a joystick in front of her two baby boys. She asked the *garçons* if their parents approved of these games which were clearly marked eighteen and over. The boys left never to return.

According to European Union law, within three months of arrival in France, Larry and the children were required to request residency permits from the state. After much online research and conflicting information, Larry began with the mayor's office. The mayor's factotum, Gwen, was new on the job and young and nice and spoke English. For a week she and Larry went back and forth on the required documentation. All paperwork had to be submitted in person at the prefecture in St. Brieuc. The prefecture was an hour away by car. Gwen called St. Brieuc twice to ask about the required documentation. She received two different answers and the woman on the line finally told her to just send the Americans to St. Brieuc and she would take care of everything. Gwen told Larry that the bureaucrats in St. Brieuc think we don't know anything because we're all farmers. Gwen assembled the documentation she thought would be required when they got to St. Brieuc. She spent an entire afternoon preparing the necessary medical forms. "They will send you to a doctor there," she told Larry. He bristled at the thought of explaining his legs to a French doctor. She said that they would also need four photographs each, their passports, proof of health insurance, and would have to be able to demonstrate that they would not be a burden on the French state, in other words, "that you have a job or money," she clarified. Larry and Kathleen duly set about obtaining the required documentation and Gwen thoughtfully prepared prettily bound dossiers.

The woman at the prefecture in St. Brieuc spoke almost no English, but Larry and Kathleen brought their pocket dictionary and their determination and managed to muddle through. The woman explained that they did not need medical exams and that the children did not need to do anything. We'll worry about the children after *Monsieur* Derrida gets his *carte*, she said. Everything else looked fine in the dossier, but she requested that they have the statement from their bank, the one demonstrating that they had enough money to live on, translated into French by one of their approved state translators. Once you have that bring everything back here and we'll talk again, she said. The translation, the single page translation, cost them thirty-five euros. They were back in her office the next week. She explained that she didn't really have the time to look at everything but she would later and that the receipt would be sent to the mayor's office in Lanrelas. And that was it. Two weeks later Gwen stopped Larry near the post office and told him to come in and sign for his receipt. According to the French government he was a legal resident of France.

Larry and Kathleen celebrated his new status with two bottles of wine that night. They discussed the uneasiness they felt about the stateless limbo the children seemed to be in. They decided that they would apply to the Irish embassy in Paris for passports for the kids. That way they'd be EU citizens and no further paperwork would be needed. One hundred and five euros, two phone calls, some more photos and a copy of Kathleen's birth certificate and the children became dual nationals. Larry and Kathleen felt very international.

They had to divide and separate their daily garbage into recyclables and non-recyclables. To Larry's amazement, by a margin of more than four to one, most of their waste was recyclable.

Every quarter a mail order truck parked in the plaza in front of the church and all day long the Lanrelasians picked up their pre-ordered purchases of ladders, weed killer, garden hoses, shoes and curtains.

There was a loud guy who lived across the road from the church. When the Derridas wanted to buy bread at the *boulangerie* they had to pass by his house. Invariably he was either already engaged in a shouting conversation with a neighbor or he would lunge out screaming '*Bonjour!*' to the startled shrieks of the children. Unfazed by their fear he would grab each child by the head kissing them ardently on each cheek. The famous French *bisou*. It took Larry and Kathleen a long time to get used to strangers, particularly old ones, constantly pawing and kissing their children's heads.

Cobwebs brushed away at night reappeared in the morning. The house grew them like hair. It was a never-ending battle.

Door-to-door salesmen toured Lanrelas at least once a month, usually offering free quotes on new roofs or heating systems, sometimes they hawked meat. The men parked at one end of town and knocked on every door they saw circling back to their vehicle to try their luck in another village. No one seemed bothered by the interruption, though no one seemed to be buying either.

One misty mid-December morning returning from the *boulangerie* with the children in tow, Kathleen was signaled enthusiastically by a waving woman shouting in French. *Bonjour, bonjour*! The woman turned out to be the director of the primary school and she asked Kathleen (they communicated in a halting Franglish) whether or not the children would like to be, or rather should be, attending classes. It was decided on the spot that the boys would begin as soon as possible. The director thought perhaps Sophia might need some more time at home. It was her not-so-subtle way of indicating that the two year-old's level of maturity wasn't yet high enough for school. Later that day Kathleen submitted the boys' inoculation records and proof of insurance to the mayor's office. *Voilà*! At nine in the morning the next day the entire family walked the fifty yards up the Rue des Ecoliers to the school where the boys began their first day of school in France. The boys probably knew ten words of French between them and half of those were numbers.

The Derridas purchased a Charlie Brown-looking Christmas tree at the Super U. For a week it leaned in a corner as Larry and Kathleen tried to locate a stand. Finally they discovered that the Bretons used cut, bored-out logs as trees stands. They were biodegradeable at least. They bought one and stuffed the tiny tree's trunk into it losing most of the remaining needles in the process.

Until they got jobs or paid taxes or bought a house (the opinions varied) the Derridas could not enter the French health system. They purchased a plan that met their needs through an American expat group. No exams were required. The paperwork was held up slightly due to an inches to centimeter conversion error on the paperwork they submitted which stated that Larry weighed 160 lbs. and stood 7'11". An insurance company representative telephoned to confirm such an unusual body type. They all had a laugh and the paperwork was corrected.

The mayor's office closed for renovations. Gwen and the mayor were forced to share space in the post office. One window was dedicated to municipal business and one was dedicated to postal business. The kind, chatty female clerk manning the post office window tried to help with municipal business whenever she could, whatever the issue. There was no privacy in Lanrelas.

There was a red-headed boy in Owen's class who was British. His mother befriended Kathleen and asked her over for coffee. They'd lived outside of Lanrelas for five years. Their house was in a state of disrepair. It was borderline camping, observed Kathleen. They called it renovating. They'd been renovating since they'd arrived. She and her husband were both retired and received assistance from the French government. They watched Sky Television via satellite. Neither one of them spoke French nor wanted to. After three months in school Owen's French was better than the red-head's. Kathleen never returned for a second cup.

The cold didn't kill the flies. The cold did, however,

exact a toll on the heating oil reserves. They called Mr. Garandel for more oil. They figured 300 liters should get them through their lease. Before they left Lanrelas they had called Mr. Garandel four more times and spent more than 1,200 euros on more than 1,100 liters of hearing oil. They had not counted on this expense.

There was a fundraiser for the school at the Salle des Fetes. The dance was held on a Saturday night and Kathleen had volunteered to assist in the clean-up the next morning. The Derridas arrived early and said *bon soir* to the people they knew. Florence and Maxim waved from across the room. The children ran off to play with other running children. Larry bought two beers served in plastic cups and leaned against the bar. The director of the school came up to talk and then asked Kathleen if she wanted to dance. Kathleen joined in the circle dance and performed admirably, her Celtic blood no doubt assisting her rhythm.

For the first six months they were in France they continued to forget that most everything closed during lunchtime. The twelve–two rule, they called it. As a result they spent a lot of time in the car waiting for places to open.

The town had no sidewalks. Still Larry felt he was walking better than he had in a long time.

There was a play paradox at work in Lanrelas. Despite being, by any definition, out in the country, there were relatively few open places for the children to play. The farm fields were fenced, the backyards tiny and the houses sat almost on top of the streets. Larry and Kathleen took the kids to parks in different towns or the kids rode their scooters on the cracked tennis court next to the school.

The Bretons have a saying that one child is enough on a wet day.

Everyone they met spoke ridiculously rapid French despite knowing that Larry and Kathleen struggled with the language. They all talked to them like they were long lost relatives. The children were perplexed. One morning unable to understand a question addressed to him by the mayor, Declan responded by punching him in the belly. After a pregnant moment the mayor laughed and rubbed Declan's head.

They spent a small fortune replacing light bulbs. The house had not been lived in for quite some time so Larry and Kathleen expected some upkeep. But even the bulbs they'd replaced went out after two or three weeks. When the power went out completely the mystery was solved. They asked Florence to call the electricity provider, EDF, who came out the same day to replace a bad fuse box.

Larry kept in touch via email with his former colleagues at BCBS. They asked him for his stories and he told them that he was waiting until the family was settled before getting back to work.

When the boys were in school, Kathleen and Sophia would walk together to the *boulangerie* to get the daily bread. Kathleen knew it was important for Sophia to get outdoors and Sophia liked it because sometimes the woman behind the counter gave her a treat, a *bonbon*. In good weather their walks extended to the cemetery. Sophia liked to walk among the gravestones and straighten the potted flowers that had fallen overnight. Kathleen thought that it was about the sweetest thing she'd ever seen.

Just after the New Year the mayor gave a speech at the Salle des Fetes highlighting the successes of the past year and the plans for the new one. Last year's purchase of a tractor for the town was a big success, he said. He ended his speech with a toast to the health and prosperity of all. A dance followed. Kathleen, again, joined the locals in circle dancing while Larry watched from the back and thought his wife was like them but different, a Goidelic Celt, Irish, taller and fairer than the Bretons, but Celtic all the same.

Larry learned from Maxim that the woman who ran the *boulangerie* got her bread from the Super U. Every morning she'd get a delivery from the supermarket, double the price and sell to the locals. It was really a bread depot, not a bakery. After he heard this the bread never tasted as good.

Kathleen was contacted by a British woman who

owned a physical therapy practice in a near-by town. Florence had mentioned Kathleen's profession. Brittany can be a very small place. The woman offered her assistance navigating the licensing bureaucracy. The woman had been in Brittany for twenty-five years and had supported her family after her husband lopped off seven of his fingers in a carpentry accident. The woman gave the Derridas two tips on surviving Brittany: never take sides and never wait until tomorrow on anything. Kathleen thanked her and started the paperwork process that day.

In spring Larry cut the backyard grass with a lawn trimmer which, to him, looked like a pygmy lawn mower. The grass hadn't been cut in years it appeared and he was afraid he'd mow down a family of rabbits or break the trimmer entirely slicing through the untamed thickness.

On three separate occasions female neighbors appeared at the door bearing food for the Derridas. Once it was twenty-five kilos of potatoes, the dirt of the garden making them black. Another time it was five pounds of cooked, still warm, green beans. And a third time it was two mason jars stuffed with what looked like lima beans. Kathleen wondered to Larry that perhaps they think we are too thin. Larry suggested that maybe they were trying to fatten them up for some nefarious reason.

When the weather turned warm and the boys were in

school and Sophia was napping, Larry and Kathleen would escape to the backyard patio and enjoy the silence. Larry read Shelley and Kathleen leafed through their French/English dictionary. The only sounds were rustling pages and humming insects. One afternoon they watched crows mob a hawk high in the sky. To their amazement the red hawk (it might have been a kestrel) displayed no aggression and eventually flew off with the crows in pursuit.

One of the cornerstones of the French educational system is fostering independence. Five year-old Declan went with his class to the beach (*la plage*) for three days. It was the first time he'd ever been away from his parents. He loved the experience and bragged about it for weeks. His *la plage* stories grew to almost mythic proportion. He had seen a blue whale and watched a shark devour another shark and he had, by his own modest admission, saved a classmate from drowning though, as his parents well knew, he couldn't yet swim himself. Owen had missed his class trip to the mountains which occurred in the fall before he started school. This loss was mitigated by a week of sailing in June. On one of the sailing days it poured thick sheets of rain all day long. Owen was soaked through to the bone. The instructor stoically told the seven year-olds that if you're going to sail in Brittany you have to learn to sail in the rain. The red-headed kid cried and told his mother he'd never go sailing again.

There were a lot of funerals in Lanrelas. The population was old and the old died with great frequency. Almost once a week the plaza in front of the church was cordoned in preparation for a burial. The well-rehearsed process did not vary. A white van hauling a trailer loaded with a tiny, almost toy-like, white digger parks in front of the church gates. The digger enters the gates and maneuvers fitfully to the grave site and begins an hour-long process of removing ground. At the same time a bright green tractor bearing a weed-whacker held high in its shovel enters the plaza. The shovel lowers, a man exits the tractor, dons protective gear and begins to beautify the war memorial and the stone fence around the church. The gas-powered roar of the weed-trimmer defeats the scraping of dirt inside the cemetery. Both workers finish at about the same time. They wave to one another and drive off in opposite directions. The church grounds stand in prepared silence awaiting the mourners.

There was a woman in Lanrelas with the keys to everything. Kathleen saw her opening and closing the Salle des Fetes and the school. Larry saw her go into the locked Café Ciel and the post office. They both saw her exit the mayor's office while it was closed for renovations. She also locked the church gate at night. They wondered if she had keys to their rented house as well.

Kathleen and Larry got into a nightly habit of

enjoying wine and chocolate after the children were put to bed. Sometimes, not very often, they would turn on the television and be lucky enough to catch a show in English. The French seemed to like *CSI* and *The Mentalist*. Mostly, though, they used the time to talk. And mostly they talked about their decision to move to France; they talked about the successes and failures, their hopes and dreams. One night, while on a second bottle of Beaujolais, Larry confessed:

"This is going to sound stupid but one of the reasons I wanted to come to France is because of Jacques Derrida. No relation, by the way. You know who he was, don't you? Philosopher, father of deconstruction, blah, blah, blah. Well in grad school we were force fed a lot of his theories, which to tell you the truth, I found meaningless or worse. And I wasn't the only one who thought so. He was consistently criticized for being intentionally obfuscatory and bombastic. He talked a lot and wrote a lot. He was a self-promoter in a sense, a showman, I thought. So, although we share a last name, at the time I didn't really connect with him or his ideas. Then about ten years ago someone made a documentary about him. It was fascinating. It gave me a new respect and understanding for what he was about. It personalized him. I'm rambling, I know. But I'm coming to my point. It's about mind and matter. There is a scene in the movie, it's after we've heard him speak, after his writing has been read to us, after we've seen him shake hands with adoring coeds and fawning professors. It's a scene with Derrida in his book-strewn home in Paris sitting at a little round table, his wife is putting away dishes in the kitchen. There's no talking, no words, just a faint piano soundtrack, and we watch him, at his little round table, a round cup of black coffee in front of him, slowly spread butter, then marmalade, on a round piece of toast. And it's simply beautiful. In those few unpretentious seconds we catch a glimpse of this world famous philosopher, usually cocooned in his own words, *living*. There's no posing, no preening, no concern about his legacy, no worry about being misunderstood. It's about the truth of the present. It's about breakfast. That moment, for me, says as much about his philosophy and his life as anything he wrote. There he was: thinker, husband, human being. A white-haired old man at the end of his life preparing breakfast. It could have been anyone's grandfather, but it was the most famous philosopher in the world. There was an ease, a contentment, a satisfaction, a feeling that here was a life lived well. A full life. There was a comfort in that moment that I envy, and that I believe only exists here. France is one of the few places where you can think *and* live. They value both, equally. You don't have to pick one over the other. That's why I wanted to come here. Well, one of the reasons anyway."

"I think it's a wonderful reason", answered Kathleen. "Let's find a home here where you can find the same kind of satisfaction."

ELEVEN

May the road rise with you.

Sometimes the moon looked so big Sophia said she was afraid it was going to eat the earth.

There were a dozen streetlights in Lanrelas extending from the Salle des Fetes on one end to the elementary school on the other. At nightfall they draped the center of town in a yellow curtain of artificial visibility. On the other side of the curtain was country darkness and the Derrida's house, where locals navigated by flashlight. The winking jewels high above their heads bestowed beauty, but not illumination. Thousands and thousands of stars. The children had never seen such a sight. Kathleen outlined constellations and Larry pointed out planets.

It took them seven months of house hunting, looking behind every stone wall in Brittany, to find their new home.

They put fifteen thousand kilometers on the car.

Human beings moved to Brittany more than 500,000 years ago. The Derridas, then, were relative late-comers.

The original plan, the one first hatched in Chicago before the lightening sale of their house, had been that Larry and Kathleen would visit Brittany in

October, find a house and begin the paperwork. Then the entire family would follow in the spring, Larry's bonus in hand, and live happily ever after. After months of searching for the right property, Kathleen and Larry both knew how lucky they were that that initial plan had gone awry. They would have bought the wrong house.

They visited over thirty different properties; once they saw three in one day. They walked through fixer-uppers on the outskirts of Rennes and renovated farms north of Brest. They explored the coasts and the interior, farmlands and forests, bluffs and bogs. It proved a great introduction to the variety of Brittany, from the mists to the menhirs.

The family piggy-backed home viewings with exploration of the region, side trips to the tourist sites of Brittany. They drove around the Cote de Granit Rose to watch the pink and red stones warm to the sunlight. They played hide-and-seek among thousands of megaliths at Carnac while Larry amused the children with stories of the *korrigan*. They walked the quays of Brest's harbor redolent of salt air and dead fish.

They saw a lot of Brittany. They did not, however, see many attractive houses.

Nearly all of the places they saw in their price range were in need of complete overhaul. The realtor kept imploring them to use their imagination. One house was only reached by slicing through fifteen feet of overgrowth. It was like a hidden ruin. Another house had most certainly been built as some sort of torture chamber requiring inhabitants to simultaneously step up and duck down when moving from room to room, like on a submarine. Other places, at first glance, seemed almost workable before it was disclosed that a neighbor had rights to the bathroom or the land on which the courtyard was built technically didn't belong to the property or the backyard, not visible from the house, was half a mile away on the other side of a cow pasture.

They did visit a promising, if rural, home with a mini-farm that was a hit with the children. The owner was entirely self-sufficient, growing his own fruits and vegetables and eating his own rabbits and fowl. The kids had a great time running from the geese. When Kathleen and the realtor went out the back to rescue Declan from an angry duck, Larry asked the owner what life was like living at the end of a road, in the middle of nowhere.

"I love it," exclaimed the owner, a bearded Brit in his sixties. "I wouldn't be selling if I didn't have to. Divorce, don't you know. It's peaceful. It's brilliant. Really brilliant. And France is just great. Just great. There is one thing though and I probably shouldn't be telling you this. I don't want to scare you off or anything."

"Oh, you won't," assured Larry.

"Well, you see that fence that I built around my property? Seems silly and unnecessary all the way out here in the middle of nowhere as you called it. I built that fence to keep my dogs in. Not to keep anything out. It's the bloody hunters. Out all the time. They shoot at anything that moves. I don't want my dogs shot by some pissed Frenchman. Now, you with your little children . . . well, you keep an eye on them . . . but I don't want to scare you off."

Larry found Kathleen and told her he'd seen enough of the place. It was time to go.

According to every realtor there was always an urgent reason to sell, always a depressing backstory. The owners, invariably Brits or Scots or Welsh, had recently experienced a tragic death in the family or were going through an ugly divorce or had been diagnosed with a dreadful disease or otherwise struck by another terrible calamity that necessitated a quick sale. Years later the vast majority of the homes were still on the market. The stories had shorter shelf lives.

Larry began to have problems with his back. He blamed it on the many hours spent in the car searching for a home. His calves—his atrophied, impotent calves—were flabby and waggled lifelessly when he wasn't wearing his legs. He worried, but said nothing to Kathleen.

The romance and allure of Arcadian living faded after months of visiting isolated ramshackle homes covered in weeds downwind from silage pits.

During one of the boys' breaks from school the Derridas drove to a hotel in the suburbs of Paris and took the RER into the city. Larry and Kathleen thought the children should be familiar with the capital of their adopted country. All three children gasped with delight when they first saw the Eiffel Tower. They walked to Notre Dame and took a river cruise up and down the Seine. The kids liked the playground in the Tuileries best of all, after the Eiffel Tower, of course.

The home hunt continued but was retargeted on houses in small towns. The dream of landed gentry was dead. Larry and Kathleen realized that town life in Brittany was already far enough off the beaten path. They thought there was a very real possibility that they would go crazy and kill one another living cloistered in the country or hidden in some half-occupied hamlet. Though they'd promised Owen a big backyard it was beginning to look like they would not be able to keep that promise.

To Kathleen it seemed that all Larry cared about was the age of the house. When was it built? That was always his first question. That it was falling down appeared less important than the fact that it was eighteenth century construction. One house they saw even had its own megalith in the courtyard. It doesn't get any more historic than having your own megalith, said the realtor. Imagine owning something that could have been put here by Neolithic man seven thousand years ago smack in the middle of your backyard, said Larry. Yeah, I can imagine the eyesore, especially after the kids cover it in crayon, thought Kathleen.

They spent more than they thought on everything, but particularly for heating oil. The car had cost them $10,000. The kids kept growing out of their clothes. The exchange rate wasn't helping either. Their money was evaporating into the air. Their cash reserves fell below $150,000 yet they were viewing homes priced as high as 140,000 euros, homes that would also require additional work. Larry began to explore how to cash out his 401(k). They were going to need it.

Driving around Brittany was quite splendid, thought Kathleen, as she shifted the Opel into fifth gear. It tickled the senses. It reminded her of her youth in Ireland. They climbed neatly combed hillsides of neon yellow rapeseed and green early corn enveloped by the smell of manure, thick and warm. They followed snaking myrtle rivers through broad, flat valleys dotted with picturesque stone cottages with brightly painted shutters, wisps of gray smoke rising from the chimneys. They wound through dark mossy forests that blocked out the midday sun. The children imagined bears and wolves—even an occasional water buffalo, according to Declan—roaming the woods. They spied enormous châteaux with statuary gardens behind ancient iron gates. Rainbows were everywhere. They saw lakes and cliffs and beaches under brindled skies.

The also passed through towns and villages and hamlets. The towns all began to resemble one another. They all had the obligatory church in the center with a war memorial nearby. Some were cuter than others. Some had more or less character or an attraction or two. Some had cafés and restaurants, some did not. All of them would have been charming when they first arrived in Brittany, but Larry and Kathleen had become more discerning. They saw the laundry drying on the clotheslines. They saw the broken windows. They saw the imperfections.

They swapped silage pits for mouse droppings. Town houses were, by and large, no better for the Derridas than the country dwellings. Most were barely more than shells with some paint thrown on a wall or two, almost as an afterthought. Larry suspected the realtor put the paint on herself just to make it look like someone was trying. One house they saw came with the compelling backstory that not one, but the last two owners had died from the same rare cancer. Unrelated to the house of course, said the realtor. Of course, said Larry. Kathleen hustled the children back into the car anyway. As a precaution.

Over the last one thousand years Brittany was batted like a shuttlecock between England and France. The Bretons were never very comfortable with any of their rulers and throughout history managed to extract a measure of autonomy through natural geography and token allegiance. Great Britain no longer seeks to overtly control 'little Britain,' though expat pensioners now seemingly command isolated pockets. France is firmly in charge in the early twenty-first century despite a tiny, shadowy independence movement, the ARB, occupied mainly with spray painting bridges, underpasses and road signs.

Then they saw the house in Caurel. The town itself, with two restaurants and an inn, was smaller than she would have wanted, but everything can't be perfect, thought Kathleen. It was the gateway to Lake Guerlédan, a popular summer attraction, making it better for resale, thought Larry. And the house itself was immaculate. It was one of the few houses they had seen that was occupied. It wasn't a vacation home or a second home. It belonged to a very affable Scottish couple, Dotty and Peter, who had to sell because Dotty's mother was recently diagnosed with inoperable cancer. It was their home year round and it showed. There was a big backyard for Owen. At 135,000 euros the price was a little higher than they liked, but maybe there was room for negotiation.

 Kathleen called the realtor to request a second showing. She asked that the owners not be present so they could all talk more frankly about the property and their plans. She didn't want to hurt anyone's feelings. When the Derridas arrived for the viewing the owners were on the sofa watching television. The realtor disappeared without explanation and Larry and Kathleen were left with the owners who kindly took them through the house. When they got back to Lanrelas Larry was so angry with their realtor that for a half hour he wouldn't even consider the house because he wasn't going to let her make a dime on the deal.

"We specifically asked to see it without the owners around. And we got the complete opposite. She didn't even run interference. What do these people do to deserve a cut of the pie?" he yelled.

Larry Derrida died because he could not ask for help.

After he calmed down, Kathleen told him that she understood and they weren't committed to anything or anyone. Larry apologized and they discussed the house rationally. They would still have to put some more money into it. The stairs needed work. It wasn't perfect, they agreed. But what in life is?

They made a low offer of 105,000 euros and were willing to go as high as 110,000. And they waited. The owners did not even counter offer, according to the agent. I guess Dotty Sr.'s cancer will wait until they get a few thousand more, said Larry. It was hardly perfect.

Kathleen was finished with realtors. Six months is long enough, she thought. She began scouring the internet looking for properties on her own. They also stopped at every notary office they saw and asked about listings. It's more work, thought Larry, but we won't have to pay commission to an underserving middle-man.

In less than two weeks Kathleen had found the

house in Glohel: a three bedroom town house with a large attic (*grenier*) and an adorable courtyard. It even had a second building that had once functioned as an old bakery. It could be turned into an office or mother-in-law apartment. The house was around the corner from the church and steps away from the town square and schools. It appeared to have everything they wanted. They made an appointment to see the property.

It seemed to Kathleen and Larry that every second vehicle on the roads of Brittany was some kind of white van. They must be giving them away, they thought.

The first thing they saw in Glohel was the Statue of Liberty. It seemed like an omen.

The house wasn't perfect. The photos on the internet were old. The owners had moved back to Britain two years earlier. Decay had begun. Houses need to be lived in. The space was adequate, they admitted. It was clean. Sophia, pretending to be a horse, galloped back and forth in the empty attic while Kathleen asked the *notaire* about the electrical system.

The tingling in Larry's hands returned.

They went back for a second look at the Glohel house the next week. The blemishes looked larger and there were more of them, but it was still the best house they'd seen. By far.

They agreed to buy the house and the oven for 94,000 euros, including notary fees. Larry and Kathleen put five percent down upon signing the agreement. The exchange rate was one dollar and thirty-two cents to the euro.

TWELVE

May the roof above you never fall in,
and those gathered beneath it never fall out.

For arcane bureaucratic considerations it takes three months to close on a house in France. The Derridas welcomed the delay; it allowed them to keep the boys in school at Lanrelas; it bought time for the dollar to improve against the euro; and it gave Larry the opportunity to cash out his 401(k).

Larry was unable to learn the age of the house. The records kept by the *notaire* only went back to 1947. Lost in World War II, they assumed. He did, however, locate a few blurry photographs from the turn of the twentieth century that captured the house in the background, so the building was at least one hundred years old. Larry was convinced it was much, much older than that.

Unsure how to cash out his retirement savings, Larry phoned Fidelity to ask about the procedure. The representative informed him that the money could be in his account within two days. Larry was shocked by the speed. He was also nauseous thinking about the taxes and the penalties and the future. A day later $108,487 was wired into the Derrida's U.S. account.

Glohel rests atop the Black Mountains in northern Morbihan. The Black Mountains (*montagnes noires*) are mountains in name only. They are hills on tip-toes. The word Morbihan means 'by the sea' in Breton. It has the distinction of being the only *department* name in France in a language other than French. The Derridas were moving to the mountains in a place named for the sea in a language little known. They were amused by the incongruities.

Like most town houses the Derrida's on Rue de la Résistance appeared small and nondescript from the street. The faded, yellow, cement façade mirrored its twin across the street. They were like two aged sentinels guarding the steep approach to the hilltop and the town's church.

All the experts agreed that the euro was destined to fall against the major currencies. It was simply a matter of time. Kathleen and Larry watched the rate every day. It did not fall. Short covering, said the experts. Greece unable to form a government, Portugal in protests, wrote the journalists. Spanish banks in trouble, announced the newscasters. The Fed initiates more quantitative easing, whatever that is, read Larry. The euro failed to fall.

The house needed work. They knew that much. It had a nice layout though, they thought. On the ground floor was a living room, the kitchen, a closet and a tiny bathroom, really just a toilet and a sink with a faucet that dispensed cold water only. Up the quarter-turn stairs lived a large bathroom with walk-in shower and three bedrooms, one with built-in book shelves. Two of the bedrooms overlooked the street and the third, Sophia's room, looked upon the courtyard. All the bedrooms contained fireplaces that looked like they'd not been used in decades. A large attic smelling of emptiness and ancient wood rested at the top of another set of steps. Their heads were full of big plans for the attic space.

Larry received new BHI data points from his former colleagues at BCBS so he could get to work on his narratives. He began to toy with the few ideas he had.

Touching wood Kathleen mentioned that no one in the family had been sick since they arrived in France. Not a cold, not a cough. The previous two winters in Chicago they'd passed strep throat around like a chain letter. Ah, it must be the country air, mocked Larry.

Glohel sits in a departmental cul-de-sac wedged between three separate governing authorities. In fact, it is technically closer to the capital of neighboring Finistere, Quimper, than it is to its own capital and has more in common with its neighbors than with its departmental family. In many ways it doesn't belong to its own department. It's lost in its own home.

Closing approached, day by inevitable day. Then the time came. They could not wait any longer to change money. They bought 90,000 euros for $121,500. They paid one dollar and thirty-five cents per euro. The rate was worse than when they'd made the offer on the house. But a bit better than the rate we got when we bought the car, pointed out Kathleen.

The *notaire* read the papers slowly to the Derridas, stopping frequently to ask in broken English if they understood everything. Larry understood that they were about to hand over half the money they had in the world. Kathleen thought she heard the word for asbestos but the *notaire* told her there was nothing to worry about. *C'est normal*e.

Out the back door of their new old house, which needed to be weatherproofed—both the back door and the house—was the *abri*, or shelter. It looked like a disappointed alley and led to nothing but the neighbor's padlocked and gated garden. It was dark and dirty and theoretically wide and deep enough to park your car if you didn't need to open the car doors. The roof of the enclosed alley formed the floor of the boys' bedroom making it the coldest room in the house. The *abri* was hidden from the street by an ugly white sliding door that leapt off its rails at every opportunity.

Neither Larry nor Kathleen told many people that they'd purchased the house. If asked they'd have probably said that was because they didn't want to jinx the deal. The reality was that they were afraid. They waited as long as they possibly could to tell their newly made friends in Lanrelas. Everyone had been so nice they felt like they were abandoning them.

They didn't tell their friends back in the States because they feared the permanence the purchase implied. And they didn't tell their parents, especially Larry's mother, because they didn't want to disappoint anybody.

They closed on the house in late May. They optioned the lease in Lanrelas through June so the boys didn't have to switch schools so late in the year. Larry and Kathleen used Wednesdays and weekends to move their belongings the forty-five minutes between the two homes. Larry had to rise early one Tuesday morning and make a solo drive to Glohel so the electricity could be switched over. He was peeved that they had to order an additional one hundred euros of heating oil to get them through their last month in the rental.

Between the *abri* and the neighbor's garden was the soul of the house. The courtyard garden and the second building, a former baker's oven, the *fournil*, were what sold Larry and Kathleen on the place. The courtyard was picturesque, quintessentially French, old stones next to white walls accentuated by bright blue window trims. It was a sanctuary. It could be whatever they wanted. They imagined themselves sharing a bottle of wine, the sunlight bouncing off the paving stones, church bells ringing around them. The two-story former bread oven building was more of a shed than anything else, but it had great potential, they both thought.

Larry was excited that construction on Glohel's

church had started in the year 1490. That's before Columbus, he told the children. Who is Columbus? asked Sophia. The gray, moss-covered house of God hulked on the hill, straining to look regal, yearning to recover its sixteenth century glory. It had been assaulted many times over five hundred years and was almost entirely rebuilt in patchwork fashion. It was a job that would never see completion. Inside, the old walls were plugged with cinder block. The ceiling sagged. It could only be described as charming if you'd never seen any other. The bells worked, though, and were loud enough. Next to the church was a small chapel. Its doors were always open.

Kathleen met with the directors of the two primary schools in Glohel. They were both welcoming and the schools were comparable in facilities and curriculum. One was private and one public. One was Catholic and one was not. Larry and Kathleen were torn. The *notaire* had mentioned her children went to the private Catholic school. They used this information to break the tie.

The last week of school, which was also the first week in July, was long and wet. In the morning Larry would load the boys into the car and drive to Lanrelas and, to save money on gas, he'd park the car in the plaza in front of the church and read—Shelley and Keats on Monday and Tuesday and a book of Breton folk tales Thursday and Friday—until four-thirty when the kids were released. Twice he had to repark because of a funeral. Once a cat crawled under the car just before he was about to start the engine and pick up the boys. He imagined the howls and the hisses, the scratches and screams pulling the stupid feline to safety. The cat sauntered away while Larry was in mid daymare.

There was no backyard for Owen. Down the hill, past the cemetery, about a five minute walk from the new house, though, was a large château that had been purchased by the town in the early 1980s and turned into a multi-purpose area for the Glohelois. It was park, playground, fishing hole, art gallery, hiking trail, fair ground and concert venue. It was where, every year, the *Fête de la Crêpe* and the Breton Music Championships were held. It was a beautiful space and close enough to satisfy Larry, Kathleen and Owen.

Kathleen was amused to discover that there was a gay club in town. It was the only one outside the big cities of Brittany. She told Larry that they should check it out sometime. She joked to him that she'd be much happier in Glohel with a gay friend, someone to bitch with over tea after window shopping on the square.

After Larry dropped the boys off at school and parked the car he watched a young mother, her four children in tow, exit a small house and lead them the one, long, country block to school. They were always five minutes late. She should reset her clocks, thought Larry. This happened every day. It was comical. On the last two days of school Larry dropped off the boys a little earlier so he wouldn't miss her procession down the street. He'd noticed her before. Lanrelas was small. He'd seen her at one of the gatherings at the Salle des Fetes. It had been well after midnight and she was standing behind a counter, rocking one of her children on her hip, talking to another woman but smiling at Larry. She wasn't classically pretty. She was sexy in an earthy, rural, fecund way. She was so young, thought Larry. Her dark bobbed hair and darting black eyes lent an air of playful intrigue to her simplicity. Her breasts were large, perpetually swollen from child-bearing. Larry imagined flirting with her. The language barrier disappeared. He imagined that she thought of him as some rich, exotic, cosmopolitan ready to sweep her off her feet. He pictured kissing her full lips in the darkness. He imagined passion. Then he remembered his legs. He tried to craft ways to get around the embarrassment of the orthotics. But they were always there. He thought of her horrified reaction when they were revealed. He'd never cheat on Kathleen. He loved her too much. But he regretted realizing that even his fantasies had been destroyed by his disease.

After they'd bought the property Larry continued to watch the currency rates. One month—twenty-eight days actually—after their big purchase the rate had dropped to one dollar and twenty-five cents. That one month would have saved them $9,000. His stomach turned.

Kathleen received a thick, official-looking envelope from Rennes, the regional capital. Slicing through the language she read that she'd been approved to work by the regional authorities. It was a cause for celebration but not overly so. She still needed to obtain departmental approval as well. And all three departments, Morbihan, Finistere and Côtes d'Armor, had their own Byzantine requirements. More paperwork.

Larry sent two narratives to BCBS and they were quickly returned as non-starters, according to the message. The response from the corporate office had a form letter feel. Modestly, he thought the ideas were terribly creative and that the suits, his former colleagues, were being myopic. He kept these thoughts to himself and wrote back to say he had other ideas that he'd flesh out and send ASAP. At the time he didn't have any other ideas.

To celebrate her approval to practice, Larry and Kathleen shared three bottles of wine. They reviewed all they'd accomplished in less than a year. There had been bumps to be sure, but all in all they'd done pretty well, said Larry. Look how far we've come. All of us. And we're well positioned: we have the house; the kids are enrolled in school; you're about to begin working; we did it, he continued. It worked out. Without speaking, the third bottle of wine blurring their vision, they looked at one another as if to say, okay, what now?

Larry fell down the stairs one afternoon. He told Kathleen that he'd slipped, but the reality was that both legs just suddenly gave way, gave out. His thighs failed to function. By the end of the tumble they were back in operation. He told himself it would never happen again.

Larry Derrida died because of greed.

The Derridas set up house. They cleaned for a month straight. They pruned flowers and pulled weeds. They removed the moss that was everywhere. They bought beds and a couch and a washing machine and a dryer and a television and a kitchen table and chairs and trash bins. They learned how to work the shower and the heat and the oven and the dishwasher. They saw all the cracks in the paint and commented on the mismatched floorboards. The courtyard wall needed tuck-pointing.

The Derridas were tired, mentally and physically. They'd done a lot in ten months. They needed a break. They couldn't think of a better way to celebrate their new home than leaving it. Kathleen suggested they go to Ireland. They'd take the car on the ferry. Nothing screams relaxation like a week with the in-laws, said Larry jokingly. They booked a cabin on a ferry named *Oscar Wilde* the next day.

THIRTEEN

It's no secret if three know it.

Everyone in the family except Larry was seasick on the crossing back to France. The weather in Ireland had been unusually good, warm and dry, but their luck had run its course. The ship was tossed by a storm for seventeen hours. Kathleen and the children rarely left the windowless cabin. Leaving them to their collective misery, Larry took an elevator to the seventh floor of the ship, a deck dotted with people and restaurants. He found a soft chair and looked out the window into the gray. He remembered being a younger man on a ferry to Ireland, it seemed a lifetime ago. Back in those days there were no restaurants, no room keys, no carpeted hallways, no elevators. He remembered curling up with his backpack out of the wind on an exposed deck. When he awoke the next morning there were people sleeping all around him. A sea of people had surrounded him while he slept on the metal floor. A different time, he sighed.

The children had been enchanted by their granddad in Ireland. He fired their imaginations with stories of powerful magic and hidden treasure. There was the tale of the dinosaur tooth found beneath the garden wall. There was the discovery of a magical stick able to break open the gigantic tooth. Granddad polished and varnished the stick and presented it to Owen. Owen carried it with him the entire time in Ireland. He begged his parents to transport the amazing stick back to France. It barely fit in the car.

The *Fête de la Crêpe* was held at the château shortly after their return from Ireland. The festival boasted of being the largest festival honoring the crepe in France. There were no other contenders. The two-day celebration of the pancake featured, apart from the ubiquitous flat food itself, traditional Breton dancing and music. The dancers reminded Larry of the Amish and the music recalled the soundtrack for the 1973 cult classic movie, *The Wickerman*. Under one tent, every half hour, the chefs made a crepe as large as Sophia. It took the practiced choreography of four bakers with oar-like paddles to flip the monstrosity.

School began in September. The Derridas fell into a routine. Every morning Kathleen would roust the kids, get them ready and feed them breakfast while Larry showered and dressed. Larry then limped with the children to school and returned back to the house to work on BHI narratives. Kathleen took a long, vigorous, work-out walk before returning and showering. Larry and Kathleen ate lunch together. The afternoons were usually spent reading, though sometimes they went to a café for drinks. They both met the kids at the end of the school day and all the

Derridas walked home together, as a family.

The house leaked. The walls were covered in sweat. The windows welcomed the wind. Their back closet, the one they used to store jackets and shoes turned out to be an indoor breeding ground for mold. Two coats could not be saved and had to be thrown away. A beam in the attic dripped when it rained. It was like the house wanted to turn itself inside out. It's not offering much resistance to the elements, joked Larry. Maybe it's resistant to us, answered Kathleen.

Larry immersed himself in the legends and folktales of Brittany. They were darker and more violent than he'd expected. He hoped the ancient tales might spark ideas for BHI narratives. He needed the help. And the juxtaposition of old and new appealed to his poetic sensibilities.

Sophia sometimes cried when her father dropped her off at school. The boys typically ran off before Larry could say *bonne journée*. The school day lasted from eight-forty-five to four-thirty. There was an hour and a half for lunch. Like most children, Owen, Declan and Sophia ate at the canteen. Declan reported that on the second day of canteen they were served crab for lunch. It's possible, I guess, this is France, said his father.

Kathleen and Larry began to drink more. Two bottles

of wine a night became the norm: one with dinner and one later, after the kids had been tucked into their beds. Larry would almost always begin with a beer or two in the late afternoon. Sometimes Kathleen joined him, sometimes not.

One afternoon Larry arrived early at the school. He could see Owen's class running around the playground. All his son's classmates were laughing and playing the same game. Owen, however, was off in a corner, squeezed next to a stone wall sharpening something against the rock. It looks like he's fashioning a shiv, thought Larry. He's depressed. He has no friends yet at the new school. And so he wants to hurt someone. After the bell rang and the kids were released, Larry asked him what he was doing in the corner. "Oh, just sharpening this," stated Owen. Larry confiscated the weapon with a stern warning on the dangers of prison weapons. Owen was indifferent.

Everyone in Brittany owns a pair of Wellington boots. 'Wellies' are *de rigueur* given the rain and mud and general gunk of the Bretagne countryside. The children donned theirs with glee knowing that a trip to the park or the château was imminent. Larry was the only member of the family not to own a pair of boots. He tried to rectify this one morning when he spied a pair at the local *Le Clerc* store. He wanted to make certain they were the correct size so he tried one on. It got stuck on his left 'leg'. It took Kathleen ten minutes of strenuous pulling to remove the boot. The children circled around laughing at their parents. Larry sat helplessly on the supermarket floor with his head in his hands. He vowed never to don another boot in his life.

The Destruction of Ys was one of Larry's favorite Breton folktales. In it a bishop warned Prince Gwezenneg, the future king, that the day his highness ate pork, drank watered wine and renounced his God (a stand-in for modernity and progress, thought Larry) would surely be the day he would die. And that his death would come about by poison, by burning and by drowning. Back in those days royalty took such warnings seriously and the prince, who soon became king, prayed daily and banned pork and water from his table. Gwezenneg married Gwyar who bore him two sons. A bigger family meant he needed a bigger kingdom and Gwezenneg went to war to extend his lands. One day, while walking through the woods, he spied the most beautiful woman he'd ever seen. She was a fair, blue-eyed blonde in a land of swarthy darkness. He said, as kings do, "I must have you. Come with me and live in my castle."

"I am called Storm," she said. "I have warned you of the storm to come. Do you still desire me?"

The king repeated her name Aveldro, which meant storm or whirlwind, and being a manly king, one able to easily forget about his wife and children, answered her question in the affirmative. She said she would go with him on two conditions. The first was that no Christian priest or cleric set foot in the castle and the second was that he, the king, must submit to her will in all things. With loins aflame, the king agreed and brought her to the castle straightaway.

Gwyar, as one can imagine, didn't think much of the idea so she packed up the kids, ran to the bishop and implored him to help. The bishop went to the castle but the king was unmoved. Aveldro entered. The bishop challenged her. "Do you not feel guilt taking the husband of another?"

"Guilt is for the followers of your God. Guilt is not for those who follow the old ways."

"Do you not believe in Christ?" asked the bishop.

"I cleave not to the clerics of your church. They chant nothing save unreason and their tune is unmelodious in the universe," she answered. And with that she conjured a great gust of wind that blew the bishop away.

At this point Gwezenneg recognized that Aveldro was a druidess (*dryades*). His fear overcame his lust and he secretly had word sent to the bishop that the king was ready to confess his sins and repent.

The following day, at dinner, Aveldro predictably served the king pork and watered wine. He understood the danger of his predicament but the druidess seduced him back to the bedroom where the spent king fell into a deep slumber. He awoke in the middle of the night with a burning thirst that Aveldro quenched with a cup of water laced with poison.

Meanwhile Gwyar, unable or unwilling to wait for the bishop to do something, took matters into her own hands and returned to the castle to set the king's bed chamber alight. The building flames woke Aveldro who fled cursing that she would not be present to take credit for killing the king. Well, the king was a large man and the poison failed to take his life. As the fire licked around the walls, he escaped down the hot stone steps blistering his bare feet. The flames encircled him when he reached the kitchen. In a last attempt to save himself he jumped into a vat of cold water and finally succumbed to the poison as the fire burned around him. The king had met his fate as prophesized.

This was all too much for the bishop who decided it was high time for a change. He thought life would be easier out west converting pagans.

King Gradlon ruled his kingdom from the mighty city of Ys off the Pointe du Raz on the westernmost coast of Brittany. From a distance the city appeared to float between the land and sea. The city and its people were protected from the oceans by a massive dyke locked with a golden key that the king wore around his neck. Gradlon was a well-known pagan, but one with a kind heart. The bishop heard the tale of Gradlon's diplomatic reaction to the slaughter of his innocent wife and child by a neighboring king. Gradlon sought only reparation, not vengeance, despite the exhortations of his only daughter, the beautiful druidess Dahut. This was a man he could save, thought the bishop.

So the bishop journeyed to Ys to converse (and convert) with good Gradlon. One day, while they were talking, Dahut walked into the room whereupon the bishop immediately realized that Dahut and Aveldro were one in the same. Dahut shouted, "It was my right to take vengeance! Did not this Gwezenneg take the life of my mother and brother?"

"Yet you took his life by sorcery," said the bishop.

"I took his life as he took the lives of my kin," she answered.

Gradlon hung his head. "What you have done is not justice, daughter. Vengeance is not reparation."

"Vengeance satisfies the soul," she replied. "My soul is at peace."

"We are born bound to the great wheel of life, Dahut," warned the bishop. "There is no action without a consequence. Just as Gwezenneg has paid for his action, so must you pay for your action." And with that the bishop left the court of Gradlon.

That night Dahut was visited by Maponos, the god of love. He told her that she was the most beautiful woman on earth. "Come away with me," he begged.

Even a sorceress lacks the power to say no to a god. "Of course I will go with you," she said.

"First you must prove your love," said Maponos. "Fetch the golden key and unlock the gates."

"But the city will drown," said Dahut.

"Trust me," asked Maponos. "Am I not a god? I will protect the city."

Dahut did as she was told. She lifted the golden key from her father as he slept and unlocked the gates. And at that moment Maponos bellowed with laughter and transformed into an aging devil with an evil sneer wearing the face of Gwezenneg.

Dahut sounded the alarm. The king and his subjects fled the tremendous tide. As the water overtook them Gradlon heard the disembodied voice of the bishop.

"If you would save yourself and your people, Gradlon, throw your unworthy and shameful daughter off into the sea. She has betrayed you for her own desires."

With an aching heart he did what he was told. The waters submerged the once mighty city of Ys hiding it for all eternity. But the inhabitants were all saved, except for the sacrificed Dahut.

Some say that Dahut dwells deep among the ruins of the city as a mermaid luring unfortunate sailors to their watery graves. Others claim that if you stand on a certain rock off the Pointe du Raz and listen carefully you can hear the bells of Ys still ringing, tolling beneath the waves.

Larry didn't sleep well. It sometimes took hours to drop off. And even when he managed to fall asleep he tossed and turned so much he'd wake himself. The cramps and spasms in his arms and legs were maddening. They spread to his torso and face.

Kathleen developed a UTI and was put on a brief regimen of the powerful antibiotic Ciproflaxin. The illness coincided with her period. She became another person for a few days. She frightened herself and tried to avoid the rest of the family. Larry thought she'd lost her mind. He worried she was homi- or even suicidal.

Larry carried a notebook with him wherever he went. He'd use it to capture story ideas whenever they might strike. Later he would sit in front of the computer and enter the concepts he judged to hold promise. He observed the sloppy curves and slants in his handwriting. He compared this to the erect, perfect lines generated by his typing. Handwriting says so much about us as human beings, he thought. Rather, it used to say something about us. In the past it was used to judge character and personality, seriousness or passion. The swerves and swoops projected strength or signaled weakness, hinted at flippancy or suggested frivolity. Now we are all one, uniform, staring at the same tiny, black, blinking cursor, constrained to use emoticons or change fonts in a futile stab at individuality. Another trait lost to time, thought Larry.

Because Illinois was one of twenty-one U.S. states with a favored reciprocal relationship with France, Larry simply had to surrender his Illinois driver's license and the nation of France would issue him a new permanent French one. The nearest place to make the exchange was Pontivy, or Napoleonville as it was renamed at various points in its history. Larry delivered his driver's license and the required application form along with a postage paid envelope to the woman behind the counter. She told him that he could expect his French *permis de conduis* in six weeks. When it arrived Larry and Kathleen noticed that there was a restriction attached to the new license. Despite the fact that he'd been driving for over thirty years, the French authorities had used the issue date from his Illinois license as his first day behind the wheel. It never occurred to them that in the United States you must renew your license every five years. As far as France was concerned Larry Derrida had only been driving for a little over one year. And, as a new driver, he would have to operate under certain restrictions. One of the stipulated conditions was that for the next three years he had to drive ten kilometers an hour under the posted speed limit. He was also compelled to purchase and affix a large red letter A (for amateur) to the back window. A scarlet letter. In a panic Larry called Pontivy to try and explain the misunderstanding but was told that there was nothing they could do. The license had already been issued. He never drove a car again.

The boys developed harmless mannerisms. Larry suspected it was their way of dealing with the new country, new culture, new language, new home and new school. The eldest, Owen, repeated everything he was asked as if he was becoming senile. Would I like butter or jam? Would I like butter or jam? Would I like butter or jam? Around the same time Declan 'remembered' more wondrous events from his trip to *la plage*. Added to the *la plage* stories was a mermaid and merman, a catfish as big as a cow, and a life threatening altercation with a giant squid. Everything was bigger and better and more exciting at *la plage*. Some might find such youthful inclinations charming, Larry merely found them aggravating.

Larry was tormented by the rising euro. When it ticked up he complained about the price they'd just paid. When it fell he'd grumble that it was about time. Things were more expensive than they'd thought.

Some nights Larry would stay up late and have another beer while watching French television. He told Kathleen he wasn't tired. Sometimes he even opened another bottle of wine and turned off the TV to sit and drink in the quiet darkness.

Occasionally the Derrida's neighborhood was enveloped by a heavy, fetid fog discharged from the frozen food processing plant at the edge of Glohel. Their quaint courtyard was rendered useless on such days.

Larry's heart palpitations returned. It's a muscle too, he shuddered.

The outside world continued to spin and unravel as it did so. China announced that they'd 'enhanced' certain economic data which would require restatement. Greece, Ireland, Portugal, Italy and later Spain mortgaged their future for spare change. The people, the traumatized masses, despite their protests, were unwilling to oust the politicians who consigned their countries to generations of penury. They were all too afraid to say no, too afraid to go it alone, too afraid to not play the game, too afraid to make their own rules. Would France be next? They wondered. North Africa and the Middle East turned to civil war as the solution to religion and poverty. The United States kept up the pretense that all was well.

Kathleen awoke at three in the morning. She heard a voice coming from the kitchen. Larry was not in bed beside her. She crept down the staircase. A drunken voice said, "Drive my dead thoughts over the universe like withered leaves to quicken a new birth!" Kathleen recognized her husband's voice coming from underneath the kitchen table. "Scatter, as from an unextinguished hearth ashes and sparks, my words among Mankind!" She stepped on a loose floor board. He stopped and said, "Hey honey, I didn't wake you, did I"

"No I had to go to the bathroom," she lied. "What are you doing?"

"Nothing. Nothing. It's Shelley. *West Wind*. It helps me think. I'm brainstorming. Got to sell my thoughts. I get my best ideas at night, after this," he slurred holding up an empty wine bottle.

"Well, it's late. I think you've done enough brainstorming for one night. You'll wake the kids. Come on to bed," she said holding out her hand in tired assistance.

"My slumbers are not sleep, but a continuance of enduring thought," he answered taking the hand.

She laughed, helping him up the stairs.

"A dream has power to poison sleep," Larry said to no one, laying his head on the pillow.

The attic drip worsened so they had to hire a roofer to fix the problem. The lights on the first floor kept blowing so they had to hire an electrician to rewire the whole floor. The mortar on the back wall blew away like chalk dust so they had to hire a mason to tuck-point the area. There was always something. Money became more of an issue for the Derridas. It became a topic for daily discussion and worry.

Kathleen signed the boys up for sports on their days off. Declan couldn't begin soccer until he was six in December, but he didn't mind because as he said, "I played so much soccer at *la plage* I'm probably too good anyway." Owen couldn't decide on tennis or soccer. "Do I want to do tennis or soccer? Tennis or soccer? Tennis or soccer?" he debated. Kathleen signed him up for both. The boys were in the same tennis class every Wednesday and Owen went to soccer on Saturday afternoons. Declan usually tagged along on Saturday to critique his brother. "That wouldn't cut it at *la plage*," he'd say.

Late under a starless sky Noz announced himself. "I am the voice of the *korrigan* who dwell under the stones of Carnac. I am the voice of the *mari-morgan*, the daughters of the sea, who frolic around the rocks of Penmarc'h. I am the voice of those beings who have not abandoned you." The word *noz* means night in Breton.

Larry no longer hid his drinking in the kitchen. After Kathleen wearied, usually just after midnight, he'd open a bottle of wine and sit in the courtyard with Noz. "The Noz knows," Larry told Kathleen. "It's pronounced with a long 'o' so it rhymes with the nose on your face. How obvious," he laughed. "It's helping me with my ideas. I've never had so many. The suits are going to love them."

Kathleen knew Larry was drinking too much. She tried to get him to cut back. She stopped drinking to help. It didn't. They were on different schedules. She slept at night; he slept much of the day. She wanted him back in their bed. But he seemed happy to be working. He sat for hours in front of the computer. The clicking kept the children away.

"Contemporary admiration is nothing but short-sightedness," whispered Larry . . . or Noz.

Larry Derrida died because of his drinking.

He hit send. His latest ideas were on their way to BCBS. Nothing could stop them now. They were great, perfect, he thought modestly. Just what they're looking for. Money will no longer be an issue in this house. Kathleen thought they were brilliant. Noz thinks so too, he told himself. They'll love them. They have to. He raised his glass in confidence.

FOURTEEN

The essence of a game is at its end.

They both knew he was dying.

Larry no longer took walks or went with the children to the park. He was easily fatigued. His arms weakened. He found it more difficult to breathe. Kathleen watched him, supported by the railing, trudge up the staircase, two feet on every step.

"There is an order of mortals on earth, who do become old in their youth, and die ere middle age," Larry said when his wife asked him how he was feeling. Kathleen said there were doctors for that.

Kathleen's French had improved dramatically. She threw herself into life in Glohel. She introduced herself to the neighbors, met with the kids' teachers, talked to shop assistants and passers-by. She became part of the community. She knew everyone and everyone knew her. And wherever she went she spoke in French. She practiced. She made mistakes, but she also got better. Larry watched his French wither and die. He sat in the house or the courtyard. He read his poets. He lost all he'd gained from Rosetta Stone. I live and die unheard, with a most voiceless thought, sheathing it as a sword.

"It's everywhere!" Kathleen screamed. "On the walls, the ceiling, the windows. It's on our bookshelves. Your books!"

"It's mold," stated Larry.

"I know it's mold," said Kathleen rubbing the blue dust between her fingers. "It wasn't here yesterday. And now it's everywhere. We have to get someone in to take care of this."

Another problem, another expense, thought Larry. What next?

Years earlier in an Andersonville dive bar on the north side of Chicago, Larry sat with his old friends reminiscing. The five had known one another for almost forty years. They'd gone to grade school together. As it does at a certain age, talk turned to getting older and a plan was hatched for a group trip to celebrate their collective fiftieth birthday. No wives or girlfriends—definitely no children—somewhere exotic, like Bangkok, someone suggested. That night the trip seemed like a certainty. Less than a year later one of them was dead from brain cancer and the plan was buried with him. Larry Derrida awoke on the morning of his fiftieth birthday beside his bilingual wife in a decomposing house in northwestern France. Middle-aged, middle-minded, middle of the road, he thought. Kathleen kissed him and asked what he'd like to do on his big day.

"Nothing. Maybe a drink or two," he answered.

Kathleen told him to cheer up. "The children have been looking forward to this all week. They want to throw you a big party," she revealed.

"I don't want a party," he said. "It doesn't feel like something we should be celebrating."

"Don't be such a downer," laughed Kathleen. "It's not every day you reach the half-century mark. For God's sake, grumpy, do it for the kids."

"Okay," said Larry, "for the kids. But I want it to be low-key, an anti-celebration. And let's make this one the last, huh."

Kathleen met a woman who knew a woman who knew an orthopedic doctor who needed a physical therapist. The doctor hired Kathleen on the spot. It didn't pay as much as they'd hoped but it provided entrée into the French healthcare system and made the Derridas eligible for other benefits. She was expected to log six hours a day, five days a week. The best part of the job, thought Kathleen, was that it was local, in Glohel. She could walk to work. "I can walk the kids to school on my way to the clinic in the morning. You won't have to take them anymore. It's easier, isn't it?" she asked.

Day and night Larry's muscles twitched nonstop. At any given moment, somewhere on his body, a muscle, large or small, pulsed, unprovoked. It was like the drip, drip, drip of water torture. There was no way to turn it off. He couldn't make it stop. Though it didn't hurt physically, it was maddening. Only drinking, it seemed, would, temporarily, take his mind off the unwanted, unrelenting arrogation of his body. Short solace, vain relief! He didn't notice it as much when he moved but he moved less and less. He had nowhere to go.

Larry received an email from Jay at BCBS. Without emotion he scanned the message. It was kind. He wanted to be the one to tell Larry. He felt he owed it to him. Your ideas, your narratives, have been rejected. You will receive official notice next week, but I wanted to be the one to break the news. I was in a meeting with the SVP and they decided to go in another direction. I thought the ideas were quite good, but they have other plans. I just wanted you to know. Also, don't be surprised if they tell you not to bother submitting any others. They've decided to hire a firm and outsource idea generation. I know this isn't the news you wanted, but I felt it would be better coming from me. Hope all is well in beautiful and bucolic Brittany.

Larry chose not to tell Kathleen. Not yet. Worse than despair, worse than the bitterness of death, is hope.

This house is too goddamned close to the church, thought Larry. Every day the bells sounded louder. Larry wondered if they weren't ringing more often than before. And he concluded that for reasons unknown they amplified the volume for the Angelus bells.

Larry started to drink around lunchtime. Alone. He no longer had responsibilities. He didn't have to drop off or pick up the children. There was no one home. He had no work to do. He'd sleep in until about ten or ten-thirty in the morning, take a shower and open a beer and a book. Every other day he limped to the nearest store to buy more beer so that Kathleen wouldn't know how much he was actually drinking. One Thursday afternoon Kathleen returned from work with the children only to find Larry passed out on the couch, unshaven, half-dressed, stinking and snoring. She sent the kids to their rooms before scolding him for his condition. Larry moaned and turning over quoted, "Man, being reasonable, must get drunk; the best of life is but intoxication: glory, the grape, love, gold, in these are sunk the hopes of all men, and of every nation." Then he belched, loudly.

The next day Kathleen asked Larry whether he'd heard anything from BCBS. Larry lied and said no.

The questions get you, not the answers. What to do? What to do? Why me? How did I get here? How did this all happen? Larry tormented himself with questions and thought in Romantic poetry. Yet I must think less wildly: – I have thought too long and darkly, till my brain became, in its own eddy boiling and o'erwrought, a whirling gulf of fantasy and flame: and thus, untaught in youth my heart to tame, my springs of life were poison'd. Tis too late! Yet am I chang'd; though still enough the same in strength to bear what time can not abate, and feed on bitter fruits without accusing fate.

What to do?

In the end he found a solution. A plan. After a week or two of drinking and wallowing he decided enough was enough. It was time for an action plan. A younger Larry would have recoiled at such verbiage, such calculation. But his work experience at BCBS, those fifteen years of SMART goals, metrics, and corporate objectives, had bred an unnatural decisiveness in him that was alien to his nature. At times it overshadowed his entire personality. He often got angry with this counter side of himself. It had changed him and not for the better. It also compelled him to analyze things objectively when searching for a solution to a perceived problem. From poetry to problem-solving. Facts were facts. There was no way around them. And the facts were these. He was dying of ALS or something very similar and would sooner or later become an enormous burden to those he loved. He was a middle-aged misanthrope living in a foreign country without speaking the language. He had no job, no prospects, no skills, no savings. He loved his family and they him. But he was no longer fun to be around. He wasn't helping. He was a liability. He was holding them back from the happiness they deserve. He was a burden. He was, however, insured for one million dollars. Worth more dead than alive. It's nothing new. He ran the fatal words through his head.

Take my own life. Take my own life. Kill myself, that's what I'm going to do. Don't sugarcoat it. That's the way out.

The paper shook in his hands. He read. Suicide. The benefits payable are limited if the insured commits suicide, while sane or insane, within two years of the issue date. In such a case Allstate Life liability will be limited to a return of all premiums paid to it. There it is, he thought, in black and white. The date of issue on his policy was more than seven years ago.

The language was unambiguous. Suicide was covered. To be on the safe side, he told himself, he should make it look accidental and predictable, maybe even tragic. Like depression got the better of me. He laughed at the use of the word safe, given the context.

Larry began a regimen of long late hours in the courtyard drinking and quoting poetry.

"I have not loved the world, nor the world me; I have not flattered its rank breath, nor bow'd to its idolatries a patient knee. . . I stood among them, but not of them; in a shroud of thoughts which were not their thoughts, and still could, had I not filed my mind, which thus itself subdued," he intoned.

And louder he said, "There is the moral of all human tales; tis but the same rehearsal of the past, first freedom, and then glory – when that fails, wealth, vice, corruption, – barbarism at last, and history, with all her volumes vast, hath but one page."

Followed by, "Ah! merica! They love thee least

who owe thee most; their birth, their blood, and that sublime record of hero sires, who shame thy now degenerate horde!"

Kathleen had heard enough. The children were sleeping. She put on a robe and marched into battle.

Larry, hearing the back door open, said, "Man's love is of his life a thing apart, tis a woman's whole existence."

"Cute, but the kids are trying to sleep. I'm trying to sleep. I've got work in the morning. They have school. Can you please keep it down at least?" she asked.

"Eat, drink, toil, tremble, laugh, weep, sleep, and die," he answered taking a sip of wine and spilling some into his lap. He laughed.

"I don't find this funny in the least," she said.

"Hear but my reasons . . . I am mad, I fear, my fancy is o'erwrought . . . thou art not here . . . pale art thou, tis most true . . . but thou are gone, they work is finished . . . I am left alone."

"You can be alone all you want. Just be quiet," begged Kathleen.

"What exile from himself can flee? To zones, though more and more remote, still, still pursues, where-e'er I be, the blight of life – the demon, thought."

"Think quiet thoughts. I need my sleep. Keep it down," she warned stomping off.

"The thorns which I have reaped are of the tree I planted, – they have torn me, – and I bleed," whispered Larry watching her leave.

Larry felt his family would miss him less after he was gone if he made the proper preparations, set the stage. I'd rather tell ten lies than say a word of truth, he thought.

Larry fell a second time. He tried to stand up during dinner and his legs failed to support him. A plate shattered. Kathleen gasped. The children wept. Larry laughed and said it was nothing. No need to worry. His wife helped him back into his chair. Larry shoved a forkful of pasta into his mouth to show everyone he was okay.

Larry would no longer speak French. He asked his children to please speak English inside the house. He ignored the doorbell. He paid no attention to the ringing telephone.

Larry asked Owen to stop the spinning Beyblade and when it was quiet said: "And thus they plod in sluggish misery, rotting from sire to son, and age to age, proud of their trampled nature, and so die, bequeathing their hereditary rage to the new race of inborn slaves, who wage war for their chains."
"I don't know what that means, dad."
"It doesn't mean a thing," said Larry.
Kathleen had witnessed the interaction and confronted Larry. "Will you ease up on the poetry? No one finds it charming anymore."

"Most wretched men are cradled into poetry by wrong, they learn in suffering what they teach in song," answered Larry.

The following day Larry announced, "Let's renovate the oven! It would make the perfect guesthouse. Sooner or later we'll have guests you know."

"But I just started working. And you're still waiting on BCBS. I don't think we have the money for it now," said Kathleen.

"Oh, we have enough. We'll have enough. Don't worry, I'll take care of everything. I know you're busy at work and with the kids. I'll handle the construction. I promise. It'll be my little project," he said. It'll be my legacy to you, he thought. A final gift.

"Not so little," answered Kathleen, happy to see Larry enthusiastic.

Larry waited for a mild weekend night to perform again. "We know that we have power over ourselves to do and suffer – what, we know not till we try; but something nobler than to live and die."

No one stirred. He tried again, louder.

"Life, like a dome of many-colored glass, stains the white radiance of eternity, until death tramples it to fragments."

A light switched on overhead. And then another. There was commotion. Kathleen opened the first floor window. The children were by her side.

"What are you doing? You'll wake the entire town," she asked.

"This song shall be thy rose," Larry answered holding his wine glass aloft in salute.

"We don't want your song. We want you to be quiet. We want you to be well. Please come inside. We can talk," Kathleen said.

"Yet there will still be bards; though fame is smoke, its fumes are frankincense to human thought."

"Larry. Please," she implored.

"What's wrong with daddy?" said Declan.

"Nothing. He's just tired. We're all tired. Come on. Kids, back to bed."

"With just enough of life to feel its pain, and deem that it was saved, perhaps, in vain," replied Larry pretending to address someone next to him.

"Wait," he shouted to the window, "have you met my friend Noz?"

There was no answer. The lights went off.

"None can reply – all seems eternal now," bellowed Larry.

Kathleen was worried. She didn't know whether to blame the alcohol, his illness or a combination of the two. All she knew was that he needed help. Life couldn't go on like this.

Larry felt he had gone a little too far, too fast. His plan was intended to be one of attenuation not amputation. He toned it down and focused on the bakery, the *fournil*, renovation. He scoured the *Central Brittany Journal* for English speaking contractors. He hired the first one who seemed competent. The work would take about three weeks. Larry reported on the progress daily to Kathleen. She took note of his apparent improvement.

Larry continued to keep late nights. Quiet late nights. He still emptied bottles of wine while the family slept. Many of the bottles, however, he dumped out into the flowers. He wanted Kathleen to think his drinking was getting worse, much worse.

Kathleen was asked to put in more and more time at work. She also had to do almost all the housework now that Larry was overseeing the renovation. People, neighbors and not, rang the Derrida's doorbell and complained about their aches and pains. She told Larry that she was tired and burning out. She hinted that perhaps he could do more of the cleaning or cooking or shopping to help lighten the load. Larry replied, "Man, having enslaved the elements, remains himself a slave." She never asked again.

Larry could no longer understand his children. They spoke French almost exclusively. They played in French. They fought in French. They screamed in French. Larry continually told them to speak English in the house. It proved difficult. Larry yelled at them often. His scoldings were followed by ironclad hugs that lasted too long. Sometimes he cried behind their backs.

The renovation neared completion. Summer began to

take root in Brittany. Spirits were up. The children looked forward to their long vacation.

The night was warm. The windows were open to let in the slight, invisible, lavender breeze. Larry sat in the courtyard alone, two glasses and three bottles of wine stood on the white metal table. Two of the bottles were empty. He waited until after midnight, and then said aloud, "But why should I for others groan, when none will sigh for me?"

He heard rustling above and spoke louder. "To fly from, need not be to hate, mankind; all are not fit with them to stir and toil."

Kathleen awoke from a dream and heard her husband shouting from the courtyard. She buried her head in her hands and shed a tear. She checked on the children and told them to go back to sleep. And then she walked down the stairs to help Larry.

"Have you met my friend Noz?" asked Larry with a welcoming smile. Kathleen saw the two glasses.

"Larry," she said quietly sitting down next to him, "I'm worried about you. You're drinking too much. It isn't healthy. I'm scared."

Larry paused momentarily before he replied. "I fear not wave nor wind."

"If something's wrong, you can tell me. We can fix it. We can do anything together. Don't you know that?" she continued.

"Our life is a false nature – tis not in the harmony of things," he said in response.

"Stop with all the phony fatalism. Look around,

look at everything we've been able to accomplish. The children are happy. It's wonderful here. I have a job I like. You have your stories to tell. Why the drinking? Why the late nights? The poetry? Talk to me."

Larry found it difficult to speak. He loathed himself for the pain he was causing. "Words are quick and vain; grief for awhile is blind, and so was mine. I wish no living thing to suffer pain."

"Goddamnit Larry. Talk to me. I want to help. This can't keep happening. I won't let it. Speak like a normal human-being." She was beyond frustrated. She didn't know what to do.

"You can't understand," Larry said with a jarring lack of versification. "Thoughts unspeakable crowd in my breast to burning," he recited climbing back into character.

Kathleen focused on the first part. "What can't I understand? What? Help me understand then. You're not being fair. Help me understand."

"Do I not live that thou mayst have less bitter cause to grieve?" he asked.

"Help me," she whispered moving closer.

Larry looked around, his eyes stopping on the empty chair set for Noz. He began to speak and stopped. Then he said, "Kathleen, I'm dying. Can't you see? I'm dying. I'm not getting any better. I'm getting worse. And we both know that there's nothing anyone can do to stop it. My body isn't mine anymore. It's not part of me. I can't sleep. I can't read. I can barely walk. It's over. Can't you see?"

Kathleen waited for a minute before she spoke. "There's always something we can do, Larry. There's always hope—"

Larry interrupted her. "Like hope upon a deathbed. Warped by the world in disappointment's school."

Kathleen ignored his words. "I'll help you. I promise. You just have to let me. And the first thing you have to do is stop this drinking. It's not making things any better."

"I'm afraid if I don't drink I'll go out of my mind," said Larry. "And self-contempt, bitterer to drink than blood."

"Let me help," she begged.

"I'm beyond help, honey. Trust me. I'm a prisoner inside a cell built by my own body, only there's no key, no doorway, no exit. I'll keep it down. We'll keep it down," he corrected, pointing to Noz's chair. "Those who came before us knew this life was not worth a potato."

"I can't make you take my help," said Kathleen rising. "Promise me you'll remember that I'm here if you ever, ever, change your mind. And I pray that you do."

"Thanks," said Larry. "But time will teach at last Man, and perhaps the devil, that neither of their intellects are vast."

Kathleen was sad. There was a resignation in Larry that she'd never seen before. Something had ended during their talk. And she wasn't sure what that was. Something was finished. Felt completed. She was tired. She also admitted to herself that she was impressed by his recall, especially drinking as he did. It reminded her why she'd married him.

She left the courtyard and opened the back door. A line she must have heard from Larry years before flashed in her mind. *Yet I am king over myself, and rule the torturing and conflicting throngs within.* Shelley, she thought. How in God's name did I ever remember that?

FIFTEEN

Do not stand at my grave and weep,
I am not there . . . I do not sleep.
I am the thousand winds that blow . . .
I am the diamond glints on snow . . .
I am the sunlight on ripened grain . . .
I am the gentle autumn rain.
When you waken in the morning's hush,
I am the swift uplifting rush,
of gentle birds in circling flight . . .
I am the soft star that shines at night.
Do not stand at my grave and cry –
I am not there . . . I did not die . . .

Britt Construction finished renovating the stone *fournil* in four weeks. They'd put new slates on the roof and rehabbed the windows and door. Upstairs they'd added a bedroom and a bathroom with walk-in shower. Downstairs they put in a charming tile floor, sandblasted and painted the old oven and turned the space into a cozy study. Larry's books lined the clean white walls. The wood staircase glistened. The building was lovely. It looked like it could be in a magazine. At least an e-mag or e-zine or whatever they call them, thought Larry. He and Kathleen acknowledged that it made the main house look shabby in comparison. The renovation, excluding decorating, cost more than 25,000 euros. Larry told Kathleen it would almost double the value of the property. It was a showpiece.

The Derridas planned a summer trip to Ireland so the children could spend time with their grandparents. They talked about making the summer trip an annual event. In deference to Larry, Kathleen was willing to try the ferry again, but this time she'd be packing plenty of Dramamine. The kids loved Ireland and made their own plans for the trip. Owen rediscovered his magic stick and practiced swinging it in the courtyard, while his siblings watched in admiration. Kathleen, unfortunately, was unable to get the time away from work. After all she was the least tenured at the practice. The trip would have to wait. It was postponed, not cancelled, they told the children, just postponed.

Larry worked in the *fournil* study every day. He told Kathleen that BCBS had loved his ideas and wanted to refine them before introducing the campaign. He would be paid upon launch, he lied. Hadn't he told her not to worry? Kathleen was overjoyed.

He stayed up late as usual. But he moved his meetings with Noz into the more comfortable and soundproof *fournil*. The courtyard had served its purpose. Sometimes he drank, sometimes not. He continued to quote his beloved Romantics, the voices of Keats and Byron and Shelley were muffled by the thick walls of the old building. Alone, in the darkness, Kathleen sometimes woke to catch a phrase or two, music in the breeze, *smorzando*. Once she made out quite distinctly, "Art, glory, freedom fail, but nature still is fair." The children slept soundly.

Larry rarely left the property. Movement was wearisome. His legs were logy and his arms asthenic. He no longer played with his children. He was afraid to lift the little ones off the ground lest he drop them.

In late August in lieu of the deferred trip to Ireland, Kathleen told the children they would all be going to the Breton Music Championships at the château. There would be games, music and dancing and all kinds of other activities. "Doesn't it sound like fun?" she asked.

"Can daddy come too?" asked Declan.

"Sure, why not?" answered Larry before Kathleen had time to make up an excuse for him.

In addition to the dancers and singers in their Amish and Teutonic-looking outfits, medieval warriors and knights (*chevaliers* Owen called them) roamed the grounds of the château lending atmosphere and spreading wonder. The Bretons loved to celebrate their bygone eras. Larry and Kathleen sat down on a soft blanket placed upon one of the long semi-circular concrete benches to listen to the music. The children ran off to play with friends. Kathleen told Larry that she could tell the difference between Breton and Irish music. It was in the tempo, the speed of the beat. All Larry could hear were screeching bagpipes. They ate crepes and drank beer under the pale afternoon sun. Declan begged for money to buy a sword. Owen wanted to get a plastic mace. Sophia felt the need to dance on stage.

Larry waved off Kathleen's hand. He thought he must've slipped on the wet concrete because the next thing he remembered he was gazing up at the blue sky surrounded by the Amish, his wife caressing his head asking if he was all right. Larry cleared his head and looked around. He'd tumbled down three rows. He didn't feel like he was hurt. He examined the costumes encircling him and said, "Men, even when dying, dislike inanition."

"*Maman*, why is *dada* talking funny?" asked Sophia. "Are you okay, *dada*?"

"I'd like to go home," he said.

Larry Derrida died because he didn't fit.

Larry sat at the computer and Googled 'diazepam and alcohol.' Kathleen assumed he was working on BCBS plotlines, but his hours were usually spent tweaking his suicide plan or reading his poetry. He was prepared. He felt ready. There wasn't much left to do. It wasn't that complicated.

Kathleen finagled some time off from work at the beginning of September, a few days before the kids were to start school. She floated the idea of a quick trip to Ireland. "The kids were so looking forward to it earlier," she said. Since they only had five days the ferry was out of the question. Larry saw his opportunity and told her that she and the kids should fly. He would stay home. "It doesn't make sense for me to go," he said. "It will be easier without me."

Kathleen phoned her parents who were thrilled about the surprise visit. Apparently granddad had found some Stone Age tools: arrowheads, axes, and what-not, and he needed help from the children to unlock the secrets of the ancient people who once roamed the wild hills of Kilkenny by the banks of the Barrow. The children were positively giddy with anticipation.

"Will you be okay by yourself?" asked Kathleen.

"In all save from alone, how chang'd?" he answered.

He spent the first few days drying out. All the drinking, even though he'd begun dumping more and more, had wreaked havoc with his stomach and his head. It felt good to put down the bottle. It felt good not to pretend. Alone and unwatched, he felt more at ease.

He took a long, slow, halting, final limp around Glohel. He noted the *notaire's* building had been built in 1783. He smiled at the miniature potted palm trees in front of the pizzeria. Faux Lady Liberty stood rigid in the plaza's center. Almost time for her to come down from her pedestal, he thought. A delicious aroma from Les Crêpes Crêperie made him pause. Everyone he passed smiled and said *'Bonjour'*. He sat to rest on a stone bench and rubbed his hands over the old granite, the moss was soft on his fingertips. He passed the mayor's office and four *boulangeries*. He smiled at the black windows of the gay club. He thought more storefronts were empty since they'd purchased the house. The town was dying. It would be a long, slow death, he estimated. He spent an hour in the cemetery. He walked among the rocks and stones and fallen flowers. He could not envision where his mausoleum might fit. That wouldn't be his concern. He walked down to the château and sat on a swing for a few minutes and listened to the birds. He watched a few *lycéens* throw around a Frisbee. The air always smelled sweet here, he thought. He smiled limping down the path on which the boys learned to ride their bikes. He reminded himself not to get sentimental. He turned past the memorial to victims of the Nazis. By the time he walked back up the hill toward the church and his house his legs were useless and there was no more to see.

Kathleen telephoned from Ireland. All was well. The kids were having a blast. They missed him. They all missed him. He said he missed them too. There was nothing else to say.

Larry put down the phone and considered leaving a note. He could confess his sins, reveal his lies. It could provide comfort and closure to his wife. It could explain things. In his mind he wrote and rewrote a note that was always too short or too long. He could never craft the perfect farewell. It did not exist. So he vetoed the idea entirely. If he could not get it right, it was best left undone.

Larry contacted his mother, iPad to iPad, via skype. He never skyped her first. She had always initiated their conversations. She was surprised. They spoke for almost an hour until the battery on her iPad ran to red. She cried as she said good-bye.

The next day was to be his last. The thought chilled

him as he pulled the sheet over his head and tried to sleep.

He awoke fresh, rested and in good spirits. Today I will not be maudlin, he told himself. "I will not be sad. I will not be afraid," he said out loud. He sipped instant coffee looking out the kitchen window and joked to himself that he didn't have the stamina or endurance to last on Rue de la Résistance. A play on words. He'd always had a decent sense of humor.

The day passed quickly, too quickly. As they all do. The first little different than the last.

He placed five bottles into his backpack. Four contained wine and one held the diazepam Dr. Youklis had generously prescribed. I confess it is a comfort to me to hold in my possession that golden key to the chamber of perpetual rest, he quoted. He strapped on the backpack, locked the back door of the house and entered the *fournil*.

It was a clear evening. Dusk was beginning to fade from blue to black. Stars appeared. Larry thought it a shame to be inside on such a beautiful night, but he didn't want to be found in the courtyard. Only Kathleen could unlock the secret behind the *fournil* door. The children should be spared the image.

On an empty stomach, no last meal for Larry, he began to drink the first bottle of wine. He sat comfortably in the desk chair, surrounded by books. The wine was full and fruity to his palate. He'd gone with Beaujolais. He opened a book but didn't read the words. He thought instead. If from society we learn to live, 'tis solitude should teach us how to die, he recalled.

No, he was unable to leave a note. But he did want to remember and be remembered. All people do. He thought his life may have been better if he'd had a biographer, someone to write his life's story for him, someone to tell him what it meant. He knew that although life was about telling your own story for whatever reason he was not able. He was not equal to the task. He needed a biographer. Everyone needs a biographer, he thought.

He drank more. A branch rattled against the window and Larry shivered. Doubts arrived. But they were only more questions. What are you doing? Do you really think they'll be better off? Aren't you hurting the ones you love? Is there no other way? Why won't you put your trust in them? What will tomorrow look like? What kind of man would change his mind? What kind of person doesn't finish what he started? What has changed?

He placed the empty bottle under the desk and began to open the second. "But live to die: and, living, see no thing to make death hateful, save an innate clinging," he said popping free the cork.

His taste buds were spoiled by the first bottle. It could have been water he was swallowing now. He peered into the darkness and thought, I have not loved the world, nor the world me, but let us part fair foes.

He soon finished the second bottle and opened

the third. He couldn't leave a note now even if he wished. Glyphs from a ghost. It would be illegible, he laughed. No, he could not, would not, leave a note. He could not, would not, with a goat. But this was no joke, he thought. It should be solemn if nothing. He might not be able to leave a note, but the situation called for something. And with that thought Larry Derrida uttered his last words, a final toast:

"It may be death leads to the highest knowledge. I shall soon know. It is certain, however, that life leads to its own kind of knowledge.

"We are created to feel pleasure: sunlight on the skin, lavender on the breeze, Mont Blanc in the distance, Sauternes and *foie gras* on the tongue, Beethoven in the air.

"We are created to feel pleasure. But too many feel only pain.

"We are created social: a child's smile, a lover's laugh, a parent's applause, a friend's embrace.

"We are created social. But too many feel alone.

"We are created curious: we fix, build, create, conceptualize, philosophize, solve, adapt.

"We are created curious. But too many are afraid."

Larry stopped himself. Too pontifical, he thought. Too preachy. Too didactic. Too pompous. A spider at work on her web caught his eye. He tried again, this time raising his glass:

"To my mother, Jacqueline, thank you for your love, if I loved in return it was due to you.

"To my wife, Kathleen, you deserved better, may you find it someday.

"To my children, Owen, Declan and Sophia, there never would have been enough time, may you forgive and understand.

"To humanity, *Homo sapiens sapiens*, I will soon be one of one hundred billion who went before; I figure I did less damage than most.

"To the planet, Earth, I recycled whenever I could.

"To the universe, however big, here I come.

"To myself, whatever that means, I tried, and, in the end, I did my best."

He shook his head.

"But these are deeds which should not pass away, and names that must not wither, though the earth forgets her empires with a just decay."

That was not right either. He'd always struggled with sentimentality.

"So sweet and deep is the oblivious spell, – whether my life had been before that sleep the heaven which I imagine, or a hell like this harsh world in which I wake to weep, I know not."

Too maudlin. Too self-indulgent. Forget it, he thought. Forget the whole thing. He opened the pill bottle and swallowed them down, every last little white one. A few caught in his throat. He washed them down with a swig from the last bottle of wine.

"Inevitable hour!" were his last words.

He sat silently and waited. There was nothing left

to do. With blurry eyes he looked out the window to see the stars. His reflection stared back instead.

Time dissolved.

Blackness veiled his dizzy eyes.

And Noz wrapped him in cold comfort.

Kathleen drove the Opel through a light rain back to Glohel from the Brest airport. The kids joked and laughed about the silliness of their granddad and the magic of Ireland. They each had five euros in their pocket, a secret gift from granny. Their father was dead in the *fournil*, slumped in a chair.

Traffic was backed up at Glohel's stoplight. Kathleen had never seen such a snarl in town. As she inched the car around the corner she saw the cause. The Statue of Liberty, dark and dripping in the rain, was being lowered onto a flatbed truck, retired for the season. The effort was blocking the center of town and tying up traffic. The children pointed excitedly at the commotion. Kathleen made a right turn at the first street to avoid the gridlock.

EPILOGUE

A million dollars was still a million dollars in the first quarter of the twenty-first century. It was a significant sum. The Allstate Life Insurance Company wired the money into Kathleen's account one week after the French department of health provided the requested report concluding that Lawrence Francis Derrida, United States citizen, fifty years of age, had died in Glohel, Morbihan, France on or about September 3, 2013 from an acute combined overdose of ethanol and benzodiazepine. The death was officially classified as accidental. Kathleen knew that there was nothing accidental about it.

Larry Derrida died because he was human.

Her first instinct after Larry's death was to move to Ireland to be with her family. Her second thought was that she owed it to herself and the children to stick to the original plan. She didn't feel she owed it to Larry. He abandoned them after all. It was not easy but Kathleen worked each and every day for normalcy. She found solace and support from on online ALS group. They became her pen pals, her friends. She learned that an overwhelming number of those diagnosed with ALS commit suicide. It was almost commonplace.

They lived off her salary. Most of the insurance money was left in interest-bearing accounts in the U.S. When Greece left the European Union, quickly followed by most of southern Europe, the euro crashed to unprecedented lows. The dollar got stronger as Europe got weaker. This made the Derridas wealthier. In their little corner of Brittany, in Glohel, they were considered well off financially. Money was never an issue again.

Half a generation passed. The children were more French, more European, than American. Owen became a physicist at the Max Planck Institute in Germany after graduating from the Sorbonne. Declan was answering cattle calls in New York City while he finished his coursework at NYU. Sophia was in her second year at her mother's alma mater, Trinity College, University of Dublin, studying Comparative Literature.

The house on Rue de la Résistance had served its purpose. Kathleen put it on the market and it sold quickly. She'd always had good luck with home sales. Larry had been right that the renovated *fournil* would add value to the place. Though he wasn't there to see it, their plan had worked. Kathleen bought a one bedroom condo in Nice and prepared to move.

The children were given a final opportunity to claim unwanted items before Kathleen donated them to charity. All three of them flew in for a long weekend.

The Derridas visited the cemetery to say a final good-bye. The gray mausoleum Kathleen fought to have built looked out of place among the flat gravestones of the hillside cemetery. It was too big, too new. They all huddled next to Larry's vault. An empty adjoining crypt waited for Kathleen.

Owen, thinking more about his mother than his father, spoke of the immortality of matter.

Declan said that he could barely remember his dad.

Sophia only knew her father from photographs. She cleared her throat and said, "Suicide—however much may already have been said or done about it—is an event of human nature that demands everyone's sympathy, and it should be dealt with anew in every era — Goethe."

"Why did it have to be our father in this era?" asked Declan.

Sophia shrugged her shoulders and unconsciously straightened a fallen flower pot on a stranger's gravestone.

In the house they updated their mother on their lives. They shared a bottle or two of wine. Sophia took most of the library. Owen was given the volumes pertaining to science and mathematics. Declan claimed the unwanted artwork. Sophia found a plastic bag in a corner. She opened it up, gasped and dropped the bag. Out fell their father's white plastic legs, a pair.

"Oh, how he hated those things," said Owen.

"I don't know about that," said Kathleen. "You don't remember him before he got them. He may have not liked them for what they represented or for what they meant. But you should have seen how excited he was the first time he wore them. He was almost in tears. They allowed him to walk and run and play with you three again. I don't know if I ever saw him happier. They gave him a new life . . . for a while anyway."

There were two plastic legs and three kids. The math didn't work. Each wanted a leg after hearing their mother speak. She was amused that her grown children were fighting over such morbid mementoes.

"Don't worry," she said. "There's another pair around here somewhere. He had two pairs made in case something happened to the one he was wearing. He wanted to be prepared . . . he didn't want to miss anything because he couldn't get around."

"One for each of us then," said Declan.

"One for each of us," repeated Kathleen. One north, one south, one west and one east. Larry would have liked that.

CRITICISM

New York Book Review

April 24, 2013

The Nooks and Crannies of *Derrida's Toast*

Jackson Croker

Derrida's Toast is packaged as directly as pornography. Its marketing holds out the promise of voyeurism. The publication announcement dictates how the novel will be consumed: "Larry Francis delivered the manuscript for his final book . . . just a few days before he took his own life. *Derrida's Toast* is not, then, simply another novel—it is, in a sense, the author's own oblique, public suicide note."

Shameless publicity is usually the playground of reality television stars, not serious novelists. One can only hope that the author did not end his life to sell a few more books. And, to this end, Francis left us a helpful titular clue. Derrida's famous, or infamous if you prefer, dictum that '*il n'y a pas de hors-texte*' suggests that a context, in this case Francis' suicide mirroring that of his protagonist, can never be completely fixed or stabilized. Contexts are, rather, always in a state of flux, and as finite beings we can never hope to 'master' a given context. For Derrida, the author's intent is not something that is 'perspicuous,' it is not to be simply read off of the lines of a text. The Derridian notion of the 'author's intention' is not some magical hermeneutic elixir which escapes the conditioning of contextuality; but neither is it a chimera. By referencing Derrida in such an overt manner Francis is invoking inscrutability itself.

The plot is easy enough to follow. Middle-aged Larry Derrida and his wife Kathleen, along with their three young children, find themselves prodded by society and inclination into exile in Breton France, far from the evils of capitalism gone wild in the United States. This reverse emigration of their European forefathers, coupled with Larry's increasing debilitation from disease and self-imposed isolation, sets the scene for a final (comic-heroic?) act of desperation. A brief epilogue explains how everyone but our protagonist has survived the act.

But Francis is less concerned with plot than he is with psychology, philosophy and literature. (In a critical nod to the third he has Larry Derrida fail miserably at creating narratives of his own, a self-referential sneer at post-postmodernism perhaps.) Much of the novel is impressionistic, the minor characters not quite fully formed, which creates a fleeting sensation in the reader. Time is on no one's side. This intentional inchoateness and the narrator's shifting allegiances support the submerged themes of fragility and dependence.

The book's heavy use of Romanticism is overwrought. The words of Byron and Shelley appear center stage with some Keats thrown in for good measure. Goethe makes a cameo as do Burns and Hugo. There is even a whiff of Melville's *Typee* in the description of the Bretons and their environment. By emphasizing Byron and Shelley—and high Romanticism—to such an extent, Francis is presumably attempting to compare and contrast these flamboyant and fearless reformers (literary and social) with his main character, whose actions and words are insular and isolating. The citations also serve to portray Derrida as a man out of touch with his generation. A seasoning rather than a slathering would have been sufficient. As it stands portions of the book give off the odor of a university creative-writing assignment.

Derrida's Toast is excellent, however, in its depiction of perturbation effectuating exile. This is the heart of the matter for Francis and the psychological underpinning of the book. The last sentence in chapter two containing the clinical term 'overdetermination' serves as a signpost. Larry Derrida—his wife and family are, to a great extent, merely along for the ride—acts from fear. Early on he states dramatically, "I'm afraid I won't pass their tests." Interestingly and surprisingly, this angst spurs him to action (Byron and Shelley again). He leaves his job because he is afraid he might lose it. He puts his home on the market because he is afraid it won't sell. He leaves his country because he is afraid it is doomed. He commits suicide because he is afraid of what will happen if he doesn't. Worry keeps him moving, like a toothless shark in unfamiliar waters. The forebodings and his calculated responses to them make him an exile from everything he loved, including himself. In the end Larry Derrida scares himself to death.

Fear is emotional, physical and immediate. Examined fear is ideational angst. It is a mental construct to help us cope with uncertainty. Larry Derrida uses the props at hand, Romantic poetry, alcohol and self-exile to combat his crippling— literally in his disease—existential fear. In the final analysis, I suspect Francis would describe the work as a novel of ideas or a philosophical novel.

There is equipoise between naturalism and realism

represented respectively by civilization and amyotrophic lateral sclerosis (ALS). Both are portrayed in highly negative and destructive ways—granted it is difficult to find a bright side to ALS—but in Francis' treatment ALS somehow appears less sinister than the evils of humankind. Without this softening and the many comical elements, *Derrida's Toast* would border on the nihilistic.

Francis sprinkles additional contrasts, symbols and hints for us to ponder. Lanrelas rhymes with Shangri-la. Glohel is an anagram for 'go hell.' Larry Derrida falls Christ-like three times. The *fournil* (bakery) returns from the grave like the Lazarus flies. The legend of the destruction of Ys. The deliberate poetic misquote here and there. And, memorably, the story begins and ends with the rise and fall of a replica Statue of Liberty. All of these skeins are worthy of further investigation and analysis. His tapestry and our reading experience are richer for such inclusions.

Readers and reviewers alike have rushed headlong to label *Derrida's Toast* a suicide novel or a novel of ALS. It is neither and it is both. Like life and like Derrida himself it is more complex than that. It is a work of art. It is literature.

Midway through this short sentient experiment called life, Larry Derrida had had enough. Larry Francis, on the other hand, killed himself for reasons known only to himself. As the novel's eponymous philosopher writes—employing his trademark pleonastic opacity—"this experience of coincidence *with* non-coincidence, of the coincidence of coincidence *with* non-coincidence can be seen . . . following the evolution or the mutation of a thought . . . ."

Derrida's Toast is philosophy, not pornography.

Buy the book, but not the hype.

InterLit.com

August 30, 2013

Edward Gosse on Larry Francis

Edward Gosse is the author of ten novels. His latest, Walking on Wheels, *will be published by HarperCollins next spring.*

IL: Let's begin, as Francis would put it, with a judgment call, the beginning of your friendship. How and when did you first meet?

Gosse: We met when we were children. I don't recall the first time. We were from opposite ends of town. I first remember him distinctly from baseball, a little league game. He was pitching a no-hitter when in the final inning I let a ball squirt between my legs thus ending his bid for perfection. After the game he approached me and before I could apologize he told me not to worry about it. "Things happen in life," he said. We were nine.

IL: Things happen in baseball and in life.

Gosse: Yes they do. No more baseball for either of us. Forty years after that game I sit here in a wheelchair and Larry is dead by suicide, allegedly an ALS-induced suicide for that matter. A tidy circle if I believed in such things.

IL: Okay, let's talk about the disease. How much did the ALS affect him? Did you two talk about it?

Gosse: No, not really. We danced around the subject a couple of times. He hinted. I think he felt guilty overtly complaining about his condition to me. I've been in this chair for over thirty years, but he was just starting to weaken. I think he felt it would be in bad taste to broach the subject with me. It wasn't his personality to whine about a bad break.

IL: So he wasn't depressed about it then?

Gosse: Not that I could discern. He was pretty fatalistic about life. It was all a cosmic joke to him. The details didn't throw him.

IL: There are those who say that his death, his suicide, was a performance. And that he designed his death to mirror his last book in an attempt to break the bonds of mere words, to artistically crossover, if you will. Any validity in this?

Gosse: Christ! I don't know. We will never know.

But I can tell you that he loathed conceptual art. He thought it gimmicky and jejune. On the other hand, more than once he expressed his appreciation for the combination of art forms. That said, I don't think it was a stunt to sell books or generate discussion. I don't think he was trying to die artistically. In my opinion, since you're asking, it was an accident.

IL: He accidentally killed himself in the same way his character did? Surely it was more than coincidence.

Gosse: It wasn't coincidence at all. I think he was playing free and loose with life. He *was* dying, you know. He knew it. I think he decided to walk on the edge, to try and experience what he wrote. Maybe to verify its authenticity. I don't think he was trying to die. He had time left after all. I think it was an experiment gone wrong.

IL: He certainly experimented with language in *Derrida's Toast*. Some have specifically called his use of Romantic poetry gratuitous and too elaborate. As a writer what are your thoughts on this?

Gosse: It works. And that's what matters. The character has decided to kill himself with as little pain to his loved ones as possible. Derrida tries to confuse the issue, confound things. And so does Francis. I ask you, what's the appropriate language for perpetrating this kind of deception? He borrows the heroic words from a bygone era to mute the horror of what is about to occur. I think he achieved a wonderful balance and it produces a great effect on the reader.

IL: Most readers have treated the novel as an examination of depression in someone given a death sentence.

Gosse: But it's more than that, isn't it? Larry was, if anything, a writer. And it would be too simple to present a clinical case of depression. It's too easy, if you will. To be sure he uses autobiographical touchstones in his work. He always did. He was a lot like Joyce, whom he much admired, in this way. No one will ever know, but I don't think Derrida was depressed at all. I think his drinking, pontificating and moaning, not to mention the whole Noz thing, were veiling an indifference to life. It's clownish. I think, like his creator, Derrida thought life was a joke and it was time for the punch line. *Derrida's Toast* is more comedy than tragedy. There is a lot of misdirection in Francis.

IL: That's an interesting take. Most people, then, are reading it incorrectly.

Gosse: Yes. Look . . . life is . . . life is tragic. We all die. And the kicker is that we all know it. There are worse things than the middle-aged death of a half-lived life. Our planet is tearing at the seams. Larry tells us this time and time again. At its best life is short, mostly ugly and unfair. But there are moments, brief flickers of magic, which make it all worthwhile. And those moments are, more often than not, led by laughter. That's what Larry was trying to capture.

IL: Whatever he captured in words, there is no doubt he captured the public's attention. *Derrida's Toast* is flying off the shelves and up the download charts. We all can agree that we've only just started to understand the book and its author. Let me take this opportunity to, first, thank you for your time, and, second, to plug *your* latest piece of fiction, *Walking on Wheels*, which will be brought out by HarperCollins next year. Thanks again, Mr. Gosse. By the way, what did Larry Francis think of your work?

Gosse: (*Laughing*) He once said that as a writer I spent more time on the author photo than I did on the words inside the book. But then he laughed and said that he had to admit I had a damn good author photo. He was always joking. I'm going to miss him.

October 15, 2063

Roosevelt High School

English, Third Period

Eileen Schaurek

Derrida's Toast: A Slice of Teenage Angst

Depressing, sad, dated and weird and probably inappropriate for high school sophomores. That's what I thought of Larry Francis' story. At first I couldn't understand why we were assigned the book at all.

The words the author used and all the poetry made it difficult to focus on the action of the story. For example, at the end of chapter seven he uses the word 'misoneists', which means people who hate change (I had to look it up, I think most people will have to). Why couldn't he just write people who hate change? It is like the author is challenging us, forcing us to slow down, to stop and step away from the story. It could have been made simpler.

It's the tale of a middle-age man who learns he's dying slowly from a horrible disease called ALS which once killed a famous baseball player. I'm sure back when it was written, before gene therapy cured those diseases, it had more meaning than it does today. The man reacts to the disease and a world in trouble by moving his family out of their comfortable home in the United States to the countryside of France. His problems follow him as problems do and he develops into an alcoholic and goes crazy and kills himself with pills and drink. His family moves on and finds happiness in the end. The end.

Maybe the book is a warning about how bad things used to be in the old days. Maybe the lesson we learn from the story is to be grateful we live in happier times. The world is a better place than it was when Francis wrote the novel. Society has made progress. We are more advanced.

Some things remain the same. Being a teenager is and always will be a difficult. This is when we first learn to be ourselves. Then there's the pressure to be accepted by the in-crowd. We all try to act and dress alike. We want to be liked. We want to fit in. Whether we admit this to ourselves or not, it's the truth. But we also want to be special, maybe a little different. As I was thinking about all this I remembered *Derrida's Toast*.

In chapter four Larry Derrida is described as an "adolescent." His problem throughout the entire book is not that he is dying from the disease (at one point his wife reminds him that "health and life are two different things") or that he is losing his job or that he can't write a story or that he can't speak French. His problem is that he can't fit in. He's like a permanent teenager. He never quite grows up.

He tries. He's good at his job but thinks he's not good enough. He wants to make a fresh start in France and really works at it at first but gives up. He quotes two hundred year-old poetry to his wife and children. He reads folk tales about witches who won't accept the new world. After his fall at the music festival he is surrounded symbolically by people dressed in old-time outfits. He's a man lost in his own life.

Derrida never considers that all people feel this way. He never learns that we must make our own lives where we feel like we fit. It is up to us. And that's the real tragedy in the book. It could have been different. It could have been wonderful and fantastic and beautiful like the poetry he loved. It's a lesson for everyone, especially those of us who struggle with feeling comfortable in high school.

The main character is everyman, everywoman. He is a plain piece of toast, simple and warm. It is up to each of us to add the spreads and jams and jellies that make life tasty.

After his "short, mismanaged life" Larry Derrida left two concrete memorials. One, the mausoleum, represents the death we all must face and the second, the bakery, represents bread and life (and toast of course!). But the real legacy of the story is his family who survived and succeeded. They lived to learn the lesson he could not.

Larry Francis is also the author of *Halves*. He and his family live in Chicago and Brittany, France.

Printed in Great Britain
by Amazon.co.uk, Ltd.,
Marston Gate.